vixen's guide to christmas

chelle sloan

To Mrs. Claus…
Me and many of my readers would like a six-foot tall real life book boyfriend under our tree this year. Much like the one in this story. We've asked your hubby for this the last few years, and he has come up short. So I figured by dedicating this book to you, it'll get done (because…women).
Thanks in advance. Merry Christmas.

guide to christmas (and love) rule #72

Don't judge a Christmas present by the wrapping paper. You never know what's inside.

1
kat

"What does your sweater say?"

A genuine smile comes across my face as I lean back against the high-top chair I'm sitting at to show Eddie, my date for the next one minute and forty seconds, my ugly Christmas sweater.

"I like them real thick and sprucy," I say with a smile. "You know. Like the song?"

Now, I don't like to judge a book by its cover. People shock me every day, and I think that's great. So Eddie, a thirty-three-year-old pharmacist with thick glasses and a combover, could be a fan of 1990s hip hop and R&B for all I know.

But judging by his crinkled nose and raised eyebrow at my sweater explanation, I'm going to put my money on that he's not. His loss. I might've been just born, or not even, when the music I like came out, but if you don't know the Christmas pun of "Baby Got Back" then I don't think we're compatible.

"Oh…yeah," he tries to play off. "I get it now."

He doesn't. Poor guy.

Ding, ding, ding!

"It was nice meeting you," I say as I hold out my hand to shake Eddie's. "I hope you have a good time tonight."

"Same to you, Katherine," he says as he stands up from the table to head to his next speed date. "Maybe we can get a drink after?"

"We'll see." I don't want to come off as rude, but I know damn well there won't be a drink with him after. Or anyone.

I'm not here to find a date. Or love. Which I know is the reason people come to speed dating events. But not me. Oh no, tonight is about work. Because if everything goes my way, I'll be adding Left for Love, the dating app company that is hosting tonight's event, as one of my many clients that I serve as media strategist and publicist.

And to be frank, getting a new client is easier, and more satisfying, than finding a date. When it comes to work, I know what to do. What to say. I know the games everyone is playing, and I know how to win them.

Dating? That's a whole other ballgame. I've never understood the rules. And when I thought I did, I realized I was playing with the wrong set.

If I *was* trying to date, something like this would be right up my alley. Because like my career, when it comes to trivia, I don't lose. And if I could find someone who was as equally competitive in that sense as me, maybe, just maybe, I'd consider dating them.

Emphasis on consider. Because they'd also have to like the same music I do, be okay with me being a functioning workaholic, not be an asshole, realize that there's a difference between outdoorsy things and outside-y things, and also need to eat good pussy.

But that's it.

"How's everything going?" I look up to see Hazel Montgomery-Calhoun, the CEO of Left for Love, sitting down across from me. The next round of dates is starting, but there was a shortage on males tonight since it wasn't an advertised event, so I knew there would be one round where I'd get to take a break from pretending to find love.

"It's going really well," I say. "I know I said it when we spoke yesterday, but combining speed dating and trivia is so brilliant. The ice breakers are natural, and you know most people are here for the common theme."

"I'm so glad you think that," she says. "When we came up with the idea, it almost seemed too simple, but also too good not to try."

I'm one of the best media strategists in the country. I've taken companies to new heights with product launches and overall game plans that have made their companies skyrocket. And most of the time, it doesn't take reinventing the wheel.

Take Left for Love, for example. They're the number-one dating app in the country. When it comes to them knowing what it takes to make people find love, there is no one better. But they've also seen a shift where people are wanting more in-person meets. People want to find that genuine connection again, and not through a phone screen. So what did they do? They came up with Quiz and Cupid, a night that combines speed-dating with their app's matching formula, and then pair those matches up for a night of trivia to essentially give them their first date.

It's genius. And I can't wait to work on the campaign to officially launch it.

Hopefully. I'm not actually hired yet. But I can read a room, and I know when I'm going to get the job. Me attending tonight is just icing on the cake of my kissing up to my future boss.

"Sometimes the beauty is in the simplicity," I say.

"I like that," Hazel says, giving me a knowing smile. She doesn't say anything else, but I'm pretty sure that little nugget of wisdom just put another point in the column for me against whomever else is in the running to get this job. "Maybe that should've been Left for Love's slogan all along."

I shake my head. "I think what you have done thus far is more than fine."

That's the understatement of the year. Hazel is the youngest female billionaire in the country. Her dating app has helped literally millions of people find love. Not me—but I've heard great things from others.

Even though I'm not dating, or have a personal use for the app, doesn't mean I'm not jumping at the chance to work with Hazel and her company. Putting on my resume that I got to lead a campaign for a company owned by a female billionaire who always gives back to her community and isn't a fucking sleazeball? Yes, please.

"So? How's it going?" She leans in a little closer, almost as if we were two old friends and she was wanting to hear a secret. "Anyone catch your eye?"

I had a feeling this question was coming. I didn't exactly ask her if I could come tonight, but when she told me in our meeting yesterday that they were having a soft launch/trial event tonight, I knew I wanted to come down to check it out. I'm a person willing to go the extra mile, so I thought coming here tonight would impress her and hopefully get a leg up on whoever my competition is.

Going off the vibes of this conversation, it's working.

Which is why tonight I'm here as Katherine Smith, the name I go by at work and in all professional settings. I might be in a fun Christmas sweater and a leather skirt, but that's as far as the fun goes. Underneath I'm wearing my sensible bra and panty set. I don't have on much makeup, and my hair is pulled back into a low bun.

Now if I were here for fun? I'd be introducing myself as Kat. She's the fun side of me. Her hair would be down, her lipstick would be a bold red, and the underwear choices tonight would be the ones you only wear to make yourself feel sexy and comfort is thrown out of the window.

Yes, I know I'm the same person. That it's just the difference between a nickname and a full government name. But to me it helps keep the lines drawn. And based on my history, that's what I need in my life more than anything.

"Sorry, nothing yet," I answer to Hazel's question. And it's true; there isn't a man here for either of my personas. "But it's nice to be able to meet people and put myself out there."

Okay, that is a lie. Putting yourself out there is *the worst*.

Hazel looks around before leaning in closer. What is she about to tell me that she wants to make sure no one hears. "I know why you're here, Katherine."

Oh. That.

"You do?"

She nods, but does it with a smile. "I appreciate you wanting to show initiative and go the extra mile. And believe me, it's noted. However, have fun tonight. Let your hair down. Literally. Have fun, and who knows, maybe find the one?"

The one? Oh that's rich. Somehow I keep my face straight during my response.

"I'll do my best."

She puts her hand over mine. "I'm living proof that you find your person when you're least expecting it. Maybe it's at a trivia night. Maybe it's on the side of the road when he comes to tow your broken-down car. Or maybe Santa brings him for Christmas. But I always say to always be on the lookout. Because you'll never know when it's your time."

I can see her point. The best things happen when you're not looking. Though I've only ever experienced that in the professional world.

But the day when *it* happened changed my life.

I used to work in corporate land. Long days. Longer weeks. Asshole, ladder-climbing douchebags as my bosses. Every day was a competition to see who could do more, who could pitch the best, who could bring in the most clients. Coworkers were fake friends since you knew they were your competition. And well...let's just say I know more than most why we don't mix business with pleasure.

The whole experience was exhausting, and I'm pretty sure for the first three years of my career, I averaged four hours of sleep a night. I had constant acne breakouts from stress. I lived off take-out, caffeine, and the sheer determination to be the best. I thought I was doing the right things, working with the right team members, learning from those above me.

Until I wasn't.

It was a cancerous situation that I'll never go back to. It's why my life was changed the day my best friend, Logan Matthews, developed a little game called SpaceCraft. What started as a college project boomed into the biggest video game in the world, and seemingly out of nowhere. Before either of us knew it, SpaceCraft became more than a video game. It was merch. Toys. Skins. Variants. You name it, we had it. Soon, Logan was one of the youngest billionaires in history, and I was leaving my corporate job to take Logan and GameTech on as my sole client.

It was the best decision of my life. Not only am I living a less stressful life—mostly—I'm making more money than I ever dreamed. I'm working for my best friend. It's perfect.

Especially now that I'm sleeping eight hours a night and my skin has never looked better.

But recently, I've been a little bored. Logan's company is running smoothly, every launch is easier than the last, and he's married to an amazing woman. Don't get me wrong—he still pays me like I'm in the middle of crisis control, but I needed to do something. Something to keep my brain going.

So for the past five months I've been dipping my toe back into the world of corporate PR through freelance work—pitching to various clients, but doing it on my own. It's been exhilarating. Developing presentations. Executing plans. It's like I have this new energy for my work, and I know if Hazel were to bring me on, that energy would only intensify.

And knowing that I'm beating out other pitches from big companies with unlimited budgets who probably employ douchebags? Well, that's just icing on the cake.

"Come on," Hazel nudges me. "Take the hair down."

I laugh, but oblige. Frankly, the bobby pins were digging into my scalp. I shake out my black hair, hoping that the time in the bun gave it some waves.

"There we go," she says as the bell rings for the dates to move. "Now go have some fun."

"I will," I say with a smile. When she stands up, I think about her words. She might barely know me, but she's right. I should have fun. I work a lot. I've been working my ass off. I've been in Nashville for more than a year now, and in that time, I haven't gone out on a single date. I've been so focused on Logan, Game-Tech, and now my own business, that I forgot the Kat side of me existed.

Maybe tonight's the night to soft-launch her back into existence. I mean, it's speed dating with men who are verified users of a successful dating app. What could go wrong?

So before the next date sits down, I quickly lean into my purse and grab the red lipstick that I always have, just in case.

And then I immediately regret it.

The first speed date is Harrison. When I asked him if he had a twin brother here as well, because my first date of the night looked exactly like him, he tried to gaslight me by claiming he doesn't have a brother. When I pointed across the room to his brother, Garrison, he told me I was nuts.

And I took my hair down for this?

More of the same comes through. There's Chad, the finance bro. Greg, the man who was trying to be coy about his job in country music, which probably means he has a low-level job but likes to pretend he's one step away from the stars. David the dermatologist was nice, and we had a lovely conversation, but then he said he likes to hike.

Hard pass. Again, I'm outside-y. Not outdoorsy.

When the bell rings for David to move, I realize I only have one date left. I'm slightly disappointed that nothing has panned out—this is what I get for letting Hazel's words of wisdom make me think the glass was slightly half-full—when all of a sudden, a wave of cologne hits my nostrils.

Yes, it's potent, but not in a bad way. No, in fact, it smells… fucking sexy. I don't know if they actually make colognes for winter and Christmas, but the scent is giving me that vibe. Tobacco, vanilla, and some sort of spice. A little fruit? I don't know, but suddenly I want to find a cabin and curl up next to a fire with whomever is wearing this delicious scent.

Which might be the most outdoorsy thing I've ever thought.

I slowly look up, hoping that the wonderful smell is accompanied by an equally handsome face.

Oh, now I'm very glad I took my hair down.

I feel my jaw dropping, and I force myself to put it back into place. Because holy-about-to-be-born baby Jesus, this man is hot as hell.

"Happy last date," he says with a disarming smile. "I'm Grayson."

I try to swallow, because my mouth is horribly dry. "Nice to meet you. I'm Kat."

"Like the animal?"

"No. With a K."

I should be rolling my eyes, and yes laughing, at his lame joke, but that's when I realize that I just told him my name was Kat.

Not Katherine.

Yes, I might've had the hair down, and the red lip on, but I was still Katherine on the last five speed dates. I just couldn't make myself say the name I use when I want to have fun. When I want to forget my responsibilities.

Except apparently when I want a bearded man who smells like Christmas and sin to take me away from here.

I don't know if I've had a thought like this since I moved from Los Angeles to Nashville. Actually, I know I haven't. Because I haven't stumbled across a man like Grayson before.

Some women go for the tall, dark, and handsome. Not me. I mean, sure, I'm not going to kick Henry Cavill out of bed for eating crackers, but he'd have to be literally Superman to get into bed in the first place. But this man across from me? No, this is more my type.

Reddish-blonde hair that's short enough to not be long, but long enough for him to sweep it to the back, styling it just perfectly. His beard is closely trimmed; again, short enough to not be raggedy, but long enough that I know I'd feel it if I ever had the chance to kiss him.

There's a little hint of mischief in his hazel eyes, but also warmth. The smile he's giving me is knocking me on my ass. And his build? It's absolutely filling out the ridiculous Christmas sweater he decided to wear.

Holy shit, Hazel…you might've been right…

"I like your sweater."

Really, Kat? That's your fucking opening line?

Granted, it's a good sweater. Not many red-headed men can pull off a "It's Christmas for Shizzle" sweater.

I'm internally punching myself, but judging by Grayson's smile, he doesn't seem nearly as embarrassed as I feel.

"Appreciate that," he says with a smile. "I like yours as well. Anything with a well-placed pun is top-tier in my book."

His words relax me just a little. "Thanks. A few haven't gotten it tonight."

"Really?" he says with true shock in his voice. "Please tell me you didn't mark them down as possibilities. If you don't get that reference, I don't think I can trust you as a human."

"That's what I've been saying!" I exclaim. "I know I'm the youngest a millennial can be, but the music of the generation to me is elite. And if I can get a holiday pun out of it? Even better."

"You're a hip-hop girl?" he asks, his eyes brightening up. "You don't meet many of those these days."

He has the same music taste?

Please eat good pussy…please eat good pussy…

"What can I say? I'm one of a kind."

"Yes, you are…"

His words hang in the air for more than a second. Our eyes

never break each other's stare. But it isn't awkward. It's...a connection. It's the moment when you know that this person is different. That there's something here to keep the conversation, and the night, going.

It's something to make Kat Smith come out and play.

2

grayson

ENTHRALLED. THAT'S THE ONLY WORD I CAN THINK OF TO DESCRIBE what I'm feeling toward this woman. With every word that comes out of her mouth, with every obscure nineties hip hop reference she makes, with every curve of her red lips, the more I'm taken with Kat.

I mean, the woman looks like a fifties pin-up girl, is wearing a cheesy Christmas sweater, and just got done giving me a quick TedTalk on A Tribe Called Quest.

I think I'm in love.

Which is a crazy thought to have since I didn't come here looking for love. No, when Hazel told me yesterday during my presentation that they were having a test event for their new venture, Quiz and Cupid, I knew I had to come. My thought was that I'd show Hazel that I was willing to go the extra mile if she'd hire me, and the company I work for, Sterling Strategies, for her media and publicity needs. But meeting Kat? Safe to say this was a very pleasant, and unexpected, surprise.

"Have you ever done anything like this before?" I ask, suddenly realizing that our time is almost up for our speed date.

"Speed dating?" she asks, but is also already shaking her head. "No. It's not really my scene."

"Me neither," I say, wanting to keep this honest, but also not wanting to tell her that my initial reason for coming here was to impress my hopeful future client. "So what made you want to come tonight?"

The side of her lip twitches up, and I swear I see a little light in her eye. "Honestly? The trivia."

"A woman after my own heart," I say honestly. The concept of combining speed dating along with a popular concept like bar trivia was the reason why I wanted to pitch to Left for Love in the first place. Because when it comes to bar trivia, I don't lose.

That can be said in a lot of areas in my life. I grew up playing sports and played baseball in college, so that kind of competition has been engrained in me from a young age. Even now as an adult I feed that part of my soul with softball in the summer, a kickball league, and my new fascination, pickleball.

Don't knock it. It's a hell of a workout.

That competitive streak has also spilled over into my career. I knew when I decided that public relations and media strategy was the career for me it would mean that I always had to be on. Play to win. Have the best ideas. The best concepts. And for a competitive guy like me, that was right up my alley.

And I do win. Well, ninety-nine percent of the time. Recently I've been in a slump, but that's just because of a new woman in town who keeps somehow beating me.

Katherine Smith. If I didn't know any better, it would sound like a witness protection alias. I've tried to do some digging on her, but she doesn't have a resumé on LinkedIn and from what I've gathered is an independent contractor. The only reason I even know her name is because a friend of mine told me. He works for a bank that was going through a crisis—a bank whose account I thought I had in the bag. When I called to see if he could get me any info on who they went with, all he knew was that Katherine Smith came out of nowhere and blew the decision-makers away.

That was the second account I didn't get. There was one more after that. And I have a feeling she's the reason behind all of them.

But that ends tonight. I don't know if she pitched to Left for Love, but I doubt anyone else would go above and beyond like this to secure an account. And if I get this job and meet a beautiful woman in the process? That's just icing on the cake.

"Is that so?" she says as she leans in a little closer. "I should warn you, I'm pretty competitive."

The nearness allows me to get a whiff of her perfume. I think every woman I've ever been with has worn something sweet or floral. Not Kat. No, this is warmer. Sensual. A hint of vanilla.

I was enthralled before. Now I'm fully under her spell.

"It is. And so am I." I push the tablet aside so I can lean a little closer to her. "I know the organizer said that she used our speed-dating rankings to team people up for trivia. How about we rig the system? Get the guaranteed win."

Her smile is big and full of playfulness. "Well, you're the only one I've put down that I'd like to see again. How's that for rigging the system?"

"Funny, I did the same thing."

"Which means we're going to be paired up."

Now it's my turn to smile. "No systems to rig."

"Just you and me, beating the hell out of everyone else."

We sit there quietly for a second, a shared look between us that I feel throughout my body.

I date plenty. Sometimes seriously, others for a short time before the vibe ends. But it's been a while, maybe ever, that I've felt this kind of pull to a woman just minutes after meeting her.

Thank you, Hazel…

I stand up and hold my hand out for her. "Want to get a drink first?"

She puts hers in mine, a spark shooting through us. "Sounds good. How about an old fashioned?"

Yup. I'm going to marry this woman.

———

"Okay, daters! You're now matched up for the trivia portion of the night," Hazel announces as someone comes around and lays pencils and sheets of paper on our tables. "First thing you're going to do is come up with a team name. Keep it clean, but have fun with it."

"Well, that's no fun," Kat pouts. "The best part of trivia nights is double-entendre'd team names."

I laugh, knowing exactly what she means. "I think the best one I ever did was My Dixie's Normous. This is what you get for taking a bunch of business guys and letting them loose at trivia night."

"That's good. Though, my go-to is Fact Me Harder."

Oh, that's good. Punny. Subtle. A little dirty. "That's really good."

"Why, thank you."

She takes a little bow, and I don't know why it makes me smile. Everything she's doing is making me smile like a fool.

"So what are we thinking?" I ask. "I feel like 'Winners' is too spot on."

"For sure," she says as she puts the end of the pencil next to her lips. Fuck, those red lips are going to haunt me in my dreams. "Should be a pun, obviously, but with a Christmas twist?"

"Definitely," I say. "Bad Elves?"

"Maybe," she taps her manicured nail to her chin. "We can do dirty, right?"

"I think it's encouraged."

The smile on her face is not just devilish, it's full-on naughty. "Claus Deep."

It takes a second for me to connect the pun, but once I do, I nearly spit out my drink.

"What?" she says innocently. "Hazel told us to keep it clean. It's technically clean."

"Yes, she did…"

Though clean is the last word I'd use to describe the thoughts I'm having right now. Maybe it's because we're now sitting next to each other. Maybe it's because that perfume is clouding my brain. Or possibly because every time she smiles, it's a combination of flirty, sexy, and smart, and it's getting me going in the best possible way.

"So, are you from here?"

She laughs under her breath as she sets down the marker after writing our names down on the white board mounted at our table. "Is this the point of the night when we get to know each other, since we skipped over that during our speed date?"

"Don't get me wrong, I'll talk for seven minutes about music any day. But if we're going to be trivia partners, and if I'm going to take you out to dinner this weekend, I figure we should get the boring first-date questions out of the way."

"You're that sure I'd say yes to a dinner date?"

She raises her eyebrow, but not in a confused way. No, the look in this woman's eye just told me everything I was pretty sure I already knew—that she's going to go toe-to-toe with me in every aspect of tonight.

I fucking love it.

"Yes, dinner's easy. It's just a meal and a conversation." I lean in closer to her, needing to whisper this next part. "Now breakfast? That's the meal you need to work for."

I don't know if my words take her by surprise. If they do, she doesn't show it. No, she just puts back on that flirtatious smile and answers my original question.

"No, I moved here a year ago from Los Angeles."

"Another Nashville transplant," I joke. "Don't worry, so am I."

"I didn't know there were so many of us," she says. "Is there a club I need to join?"

"Nah. It's just a badge of honor we wear that pisses off the locals. Especially when they find out I'm from Connecticut."

She covers her heart and feigns a mocking shock. "Why, I do declare. A Yankee? In Nashville?"

It's really unfair that she's beautiful, has impeccable music taste, and funny. I don't stand a fucking chance of not falling for this woman. "You know, for not being from the South, you do that accent pretty well."

She takes a small bow. "In my short time here, I've become enmeshed with my fair share of born-and-bred Tennesseans. I've picked up a few things along the way."

"And they don't give you shit for being from California?"

She shakes her head. "Not this group. I've been really lucky to meet some amazing people. I was hesitant to move here, but they made me feel welcomed."

"Did you come here for work?"

She nods, but doesn't elaborate. "You?"

"Same," I say. "My company has offices in New York, which is where I started as an underling. But three years ago, I got promoted, which came with a move here. And I figured, why not? I was still in my twenties. I'd never lived outside of the Northeast before, so if I was ever going to move, that was the time."

"I get it," she says. "We're only young once."

"Cheers to that," I say as we each raise our drinks in a toast. "To transplants and unexpected meetings."

She smiles as she taps her glass against mine. "To winning trivia and hopefully more."

We share a look and a smile as we take sips of our drinks. I want to keep getting to know her—what she does, more of her interests. Really, wherever the conversation will go, but when we set our drinks down, the emcee gets on the mic to start going over the directions for the game.

It's fine. We have all night. And hopefully, many more nights after this.

"So do you have any specialty categories that I can take a backseat on?" I ask.

She shrugs, but I can tell she's trying to be nonchalant. "I'm pretty well-rounded. Not great with sports, but I can hold my own."

"Don't worry. I've got us covered on that."

She raises her eyebrow. "Are you one of those sports guys who makes it their whole entire personality and can rattle off random stats from random days and random years that are supposed to impress women? Because I'll give you a hint; it won't impress me. At all."

I laugh, knowing exactly what kind of guy she's talking about. And I know that because those guys are my best friends. "I could be, but I'm not."

She sits back a little, trying to assess me. I let her, sitting back myself, and if she's going to give me a onceover, why would I not use the chance to take her in?

She's fucking stunning. I've always been a sucker for a woman with curves, and Kat has plenty of them in all the right spots. She might be wearing a ridiculous sweater, but that's not hiding what I know is underneath. The leather skirt and knee-high boots have my mouth watering. And that lipstick? What I wouldn't give for it to stain my cock.

Add all of that with her quick wit? The woman is a vixen. In the best way possible.

"Okay, so let me take a stab at who Grayson is," she says confidently. "From Connecticut, so I'm going to guess that you went to some fancy private school and a private college. You said that your company has offices in multiple cities, so you're some kind of finance or business bro. You know sports, so you probably played a sport in college. Am I doing well so far?"

I have to laugh, because she's fucking nailing it. "Can I have a turn now? Since you absolutely clocked me."

She makes a motion, signaling she's an open book.

"I'm going to guess you're something in the legal business," I say. "Sharp mind. Quick comebacks. Definitely some sort of liti-gator. You like old school hip-hop, so you're an old soul. You drink old fashioneds, so you aren't a typical girly girl. But the boots and skirt tell me you still like to be feminine."

She shakes her head and pats my hand for good measure. "Close on a few. So far in the others…"

I'm now wondering what I was wrong on, but with impeccable timing, the emcee announces the first question.

"Question one, and we're going to start easy with a general Christmas theme: What was Frosty the Snowman's pipe made of?"

Kat and I look at each other and equally roll our eyes. If this is going to be the difficulty level all night, we're going to run away with this.

"Just so you know," she says as she writes down our answer. "*Frosty* is without a doubt the best Christmas movie of them all."

"Oh, I beg to differ. That correct answer would be *Rudolph*."

She hands our slip of paper to the assistant coming around to collect them. "It's good, but I never got the reason why he wanted to be a dentist. Seemed very out of pocket."

"Which is the beauty of it. Don't you appreciate the unexpected?"

She thinks about it for a second before we lock eyes. "You know what, I do."

Our gaze holds for a few seconds, something passing between us that I know we both feel.

What the hell is going on? I've been instantly attracted to women before. I've felt a spark. But what is flowing between Kat and me now is a full-on five-alarm fire.

As the game goes along, we get every one right. Some from me, some from her. A few we've shared a knowing look. I know I wasn't planning on treating this like a date tonight, but the more and more time I spend with this woman, the more I'm forgetting that work was the primary objective.

"Question number six, category, video games. What is the name of the video game that is currently the number-one game in the world due to its new Christmas variation?"

I hear Kat chuckle as she takes the answer sheet and pencil in her hand.

"You know the answer?" She nods, and the smile on her face makes me feel like I'm missing out on the inside joke. "You're a video game girl?"

Is that what she meant when she said earlier that I was way off? I mean, I play some. Mostly sports games and a few super-popular ones, but I'm not what you'd consider a gamer. I definitely would've had no clue what this answer would've been.

"I wouldn't say that," she says, and as I spy over her shoulder I see she writes the name SpaceCraft. "Let's just say that when it comes to video games, I'm not going to be wrong. Especially this game."

"Pencils down," the emcee announces before his assistant comes around to collect our answers. "If you answered Space-Craft, congratulations, you're right!"

There are more groans than cheers after that, but it's all celebration for Kat and I.

"How the hell did you know that?" I ask as the emcee starts announcing the scores. I don't need to listen because I know we're in first place.

"My best friend…let's just say he's a video game nut."

He? I wasn't expecting that answer.

She gives me a raised eyebrow. "Are you going to be one of those guys that can't handle that my best friend is a man?"

I quickly think about it, because I've never been in this situation before. "No. Just wasn't expecting it. Took me off guard."

"I get that," she says as she picks up her drink. "But I can assure you, we've never dated. Kissed once, and it was gross. But that was back in college. We were roommates when we graduated, but long ago started living our separate lives. Now I work for him and occasionally run his life."

"Interesting," I say. "What kind of work is it you do?"

Kat opens her mouth to answer me, but yet again, before she can say anything, the emcee announces our next question.

"Category: Movies. What famous movie had the line, 'shitter's full'?"

I look over to Kat, who shares a knowing smile with me. A woman who knows *National Lampoon*? I don't know if she can get more perfect.

Unfortunately, the questions get a little more difficult as the night goes along. We lose a couple, but thank God Kat is some kind of Christmas movie trivia savant. The ones we didn't know came in the carol category—who the hell was supposed to know the original name of "The Little Drummer Boy"—and no one in the bar knew who the political cartoonist was who coined the image of the modern-day Santa Claus. But I can tell by the way Kat's locking in on every answer, and how I'm matching her with most questions, that we're not going to lose.

It's fucking hot as hell.

"Okay, everyone, final round," the emcee announces. "To make things interesting, pairs need to decide how many points they want to wager. And, you must lock in your wager before I read the question. Category: Movies."

We share a look, but from the determination in her eyes, I know what she's going to say.

"All in."

Two words. Two words that are not supposed to be sexy, yet somehow are the hottest thing she could've said in that moment.

I reach out for her hand, and thank God she doesn't move away as I lace my fingers in hers. "It's all you. Bring it home."

"Oh, I should've told you one stipulation," the emcee says. "This question is going to have a closest-to-the-correct-answer caveat, as it's a specific number without multiple choice options. Closest to the correct answer without going over wins. But! If someone guesses it on the nose, despite how many points are wagered, they will automatically win the game."

"The fuck!" Kat jumps out of her chair, and sure, a few tables turn to us and give her a sideways glance, but I'm just laughing. Because even though she said it, I was thinking about it.

"Easy now," I say, pulling her back down. "Plus, they don't stand a chance. You got this."

"Fuck yes, I do," she says, which just makes me laugh more. "All right, trivia boy. Bring it!"

I don't know if he heard her, but the emcee does just that.

"The final question of the night! In the movie "White Christmas," how many times is the word 'general' said in the movie?"

A hush goes through the crowd. I look around, and a few people who looked confident thirty seconds ago suddenly look worried.

Except Kat. The smile on her face right now is downright diabolical.

Oh, we're gonna win…

"Nineteen? That's it?" I ask as I look over her shoulder to see what she's writing. "I feel like a trivia question like that would be bigger."

She shakes her head as she underlines the answer for extra emphasis. "That's the point. There's a whole song about the General, so people think it's more than it really is."

"And how do you know the number?"

"White Christmas drinking game," she says as she folds up her answer to hand in. "Some families run 5Ks during holidays. Some families drink. Mine drinks."

I chuckle under my breath and look in awe at Kat as she sits up a little taller, confident in her answer.

"Folks! We have an exact answer, but it didn't matter for the automatic win because they were ahead the whole game. Your winners tonight, Claus Deep!"

"Woo!" Kat screeches, jumping up from her chair and celebrating. I join her, but I choose a fist pump. Much more manly.

I turn toward her, ready to say congratulations, when she throws her arms around my neck.

"Best partner ever!" she cries out as she hugs herself into me. I return the sentiment, bringing her in close.

Fuck, she feels good. Too good. So good I don't want to let go.

Actually, I don't want this night to end. Sure, I can get her number. I'm sure Hazel is sending responses to people who matched so we can connect that way. But I don't want to wait.

"Hey," I say as I brush my hands over her arms. "Want to keep this night going?"

Sure, I could've used some sort of line. Or been smoother about it. But I have a feeling Kat is a woman who appreciates the directness.

The grin on her face says that I'm right.

"What do you have in mind?"

I put my hand on the small of her back, leading her out of the bar. "I have a few ideas."

guide to christmas (and love) rule #53

There's no such thing as a perfect Christmas present. Even if he eats pussy and owns a dog.

3

kat

Fuck, I like this guy.

I really, really, like this guy.

Like I need to not like this guy the way I like this guy.

Okay, maybe that's not the way to describe it. There's no *need* for me to not like him. He's good looking. Smart. Funny. The vibes have been there since the moment he sat down across from me. I'm not sure exactly what he does for work, but judging by the drinks he's ordered, and the liquor he's asked them to make it with, while also paired with his expensive watch and designer jeans, I'm going to say he's doing well for himself.

The Katherine part of my brain is saying he's checking off all the early boxes. But Katherine is also an overthinker and remembers the last time a good-looking man who wore expensive clothes and smelled like sin and seduction came walking into my life.

It was bad. Very bad. It ended bad, and it's the reason for most of my trust issues.

Yet as Grayson comes walking back over with our drinks, me, right now as Kat, is telling Katherine to fuck all the way off. Because the way he's holding himself, the slight grin on his handsome face, and the fact that he's giving me a forearm show as he has his sleeves pushed up, the thoughts I'm having are purely Kat thoughts.

They're dirty. So fucking dirty.

"Here we are, one gingerbread old fashioned," Grayson says, placing my drink at the table we found at a cute pop-up holiday bar just off Broadway. We didn't mean to come here, but we couldn't help it when we walked past, saw the fun ambiance, and then heard the music the DJ was playing. "Shall we make a toast?"

I pick up my drink and lean into him. Because even though my Katherine brain is telling me to be cautious, my Kat body is clearly operating by the motto of "I'll do whatever the fuck I want."

"I think it's a rule you have to."

"To holiday magic," he says.

"And to the presents you didn't expect to get."

We share a smile and tap our glasses, each of us taking a delicate sip of the—

"Damn, this is good!" I exclaim.

Luckily, my outburst only makes him laugh. "You don't hold back your feelings, do you?"

I laugh as I put down the rocks glass. "Oh, I'm a straight shooter. I can have a poker face, but if you ask me what I'm thinking, I'm not going to mince words. It's a blessing and a curse."

"I think it's a blessing," he says. "You always know where you stand with someone."

I playfully wag my finger at him. "You say that now, then one day you're asking me a question and you don't like the answer, and then boom! You never call me again."

This makes him smile. "I like the idea of calling you at any point."

Interesting he took that part of the conversation to pick up on. I could tell this man was riding the line between cocky asshole and confident man from the second he sat down. That's probably why the Katherine part of my brain started sending small red alerts. Because this guy is my type, through and through. And the cockier he is, the more attracted I am. It's a character flaw.

"We're just assuming that I'm going to give you my number?"

The challenging looks we're giving to each other right now, the ones filled with determination, but also a little lust…this is why I like cocky men. Because I'm a cocky girl. Both Kat and Katherine. And if the banter and the sparring is there… Well, there's nothing hotter.

"I'm not assuming," he says as he leans a little closer. "But I calculated the odds, and I think when it comes to leaving here with your number, my chances are pretty high."

"You're a betting man?"

He nods as his hand "slips" down to brush the top of mine. I must say, it was a good move. "A blackjack table hates to see me coming."

"I'm more of a craps girl myself."

I swear at that moment, I see an actual spark of fire ignite in his eye. "Not an easy game."

"It's all about the strategy," I say. "Which is my forte."

"I like it," he says as he continues to brush his fingers over my hand. With every touch, and every swoop, I swear a new goosebump pops up somewhere on my body. "What else would you consider your fortes?"

Check box for Katherine: He's asking questions about me. Not domineering the conversation.

Check box for Kat: God, he smells fucking good.

"Let's see, as you saw earlier, my trivia skills are unmatched. I'm fluent in French, and I can name most tunes in less than five notes. Well, anything released before 2020."

"It's when the best music was developed."

"I couldn't agree more," I say. "Oh, and my career. I know

everyone thinks, or wants, to be the best at their job, but I really am."

Grayson has been showing interest with everything I'm saying. But I swear, at this moment, he's maybe more turned on than ever.

"Really? A very rare pairing to have two people who are dominating in their career fields meet up."

"I believe it's what the business world calls a 'power couple.'"

"I've always wanted to be in one of those," he says. "So, what field do you dominate in?"

Just as I'm about to tell him about my job in media strategies —and the very unconventional way that I've taken my career— the DJ changes the song and both of our eyes light up.

"What about dancing?" he asks. "Is that a forte?"

I subtly shake my head. "Not really. I'm not horrible at it, but I wouldn't put it on my top list of special skills."

"Well, I do," he says, standing up and holding out his hand. "Let's put those skills on display."

Fuck, he can dance, too? I'm going to have sex tonight, aren't I?

"I'm going to warn you, I'm not trying to be coy," I say as I give him my hand. "I'm really not much of a dancer."

"We'll see about that."

Grayson leads me to the dance floor of the bar, which is packed with people who are all dressed as festively as the bar is decorated. It's a good excuse for Grayson to pull me closer, both of our hands now linked as we start feeling the beat of the music.

He wasn't lying. He is good. His hips are subtly moving to every beat perfectly—the slight bounce of his shoulders, the way he leads me with his hands without being forceful, all while staying on perfect beat.

It's fucking sexy.

"So we have this forte," I say. "What are some others I need to be aware about?"

"Well," he says as he changes his hand position, bringing our joined ones to the small of my back so he can bring me in closer. To some the move might feel a little bold, but not to me. I fucking love it. "I also have my career. Baseball. And, my hidden talent, that very few people know about, is that I can play the piano. Pretty well, actually."

I wasn't expecting that one. "Really? How long?"

"Since I was a kid," he says. "My mother was insistent that we all did something in the fine arts, at least until we were in high school. My sister danced. My older brother took up art. And me? Piano, for some reason, called my name. My grandparents had one, and I loved plonking away on it. I quit taking lessons and seriously playing in high school, but if I saw one today, I'm sure I could whip a little something up."

"When I see videos of piano players playing something classical, then it switches to a rap song, I'm always amazed."

This makes him smile. "Funny you say that, because that specific kind of music, that's also my forte."

We share a smile in the silence, but it's not awkward. Not at all. Yes, there are a million more questions we could ask each other. But as the song changes from the fast and upbeat song we were just dancing along with to a slower, more sensual song, neither of us feel the need to fill in the silence. Instead, I wrap my arms around his neck as he pulls me in tighter, both of us just feeling the beat of the music between us.

This is not how I expected this night to go. If I would've put a prediction on my evening, I'd have put all my money in on by this time I'd already be home. That I would've made a beeline for the exit the second trivia was over, picked up some Taco Bell on the way home—because Taco Bell is elite and I'll hear no arguments against it—and I'd be sitting in front of the television, watching the latest episode of reality trash television that's my dirty little secret while enjoying a Baja Blast.

But here I am. I let Kat take over for just a little bit tonight, and I'm now dancing with a handsome man who's making me think and feel things I was beginning to believe I left in Los Angeles.

The music comes to a stop, but neither of us pull away. The DJ announces that it's last call at the bar, which makes my stomach sink. I'm not ready for this night to end. Not yet.

"Want to go one more place?" I ask.

His smile is instant. "What do you have in mind?"

———

"Hot dogs?"

I look over my shoulder to Grayson, who's just looking at me with a smirk. "Yes hot dogs. I'm hungry, and they're right here."

We step up in line and each order two—mine with ketchup and relish, his with mustard and sauerkraut.

"You know, for our first dinner together, I thought it would be somewhere fancier. Cloth napkins. Good bourbon. You in a dress that would drive me crazy."

I smile as we step aside to wait for our order. "That can happen. Just this first."

He casually reaches for my hand, linking our fingers together as we talk about more of nothing as we wait for our order. Once our food is secured, we head down to the river, finding benches that overlook the Cumberland. It's the perfect spot to end a perfect night.

"Okay, I know I was teasing earlier, but this is absolutely hitting the spot," he says as he takes a big bite out of his dog. "These get a lot of hate, but I love a good hot dog."

"For sure," I say as I also take a bite of mine. "Plus, it's the perfect gateway for the best ice breaker debate of all time."

His face turns into pure excitement. "Are you talking about the age-old debate if a hot dog is a sandwich?"

"I am," I say. "Now, be very careful with your answer. I'd hate for you to lose points at this critical stage of the night."

"No need to be careful, because I'm right," he says. "It's a sandwich, in the sense that it's in the sandwich family. There's meat and bread. However, it's like a dolphin being a mammal. Technically it is, but is that what you really think of when you say 'name a mammal?' No, therefore the answer is yes, but with a disclaimer."

I feel my mouth dropping. I didn't know there could be a perfect answer to that question, but there it is. And not only is it perfectly worded, it's exactly what I think.

This man is too good to be true. He's so good that even the Katherine portion of my brain is starting to loosen the grip on her panties. And that never happens.

"I take it I didn't lose any points?" he says with a smirk.

"I'm impressed." I do my best to recover from my shock, but I don't know if it works. "So you're a piano-playing, trivia-winning, dancing king who, let me guess, volunteers on the weekends building houses?"

He laughs and shakes his head. "No building houses. But I do go to the animal shelter and walk the dogs there."

Oh, fuck my life. If I see him with a puppy, I'm going to let him put it in every hole.

"Okay, then, what gives?" I ask, because Katherine is not going to let me sleep with him tonight if I don't. "What's wrong with you?"

He almost spits out his bite at my directness. "You really don't pull punches, do you?"

"Never have, never will," I say. "But I'm assuming if you're at a speed dating event, you're single. At least, I hope you are."

"Very," he says. "Cheating is an absolute no for me."

"I'm glad we're on the same page about that," I say. "Okay, so the question now begs to be asked, why are you single?"

I hate getting that question more than any others in the dating world. But I can't not ask it tonight. This man is just too… I don't want to say the word perfect, because no one is, but Grayson is inching damn close to that line.

"I'm honestly not sure," he says. "I've dated some since I

moved here. A few more serious than others. My motto is why waste time dating if you know it's probably not going to be for the long haul?"

"I completely agree," I say. "Time is a commodity. And in my world, you have to earn my time."

"Exactly." We're both done with our hot dogs, which gives Grayson the opportunity to move closer to me, his arm naturally going around the back of the bench. "Plus, we've just been talking about our good qualities. We haven't disclosed the bads yet."

I know what he means, but the flirtatious tone of his voice is still making me think what he's about to say are pink flags at best.

"You're very right," I say, wondering what I want to tell him about myself that's true, but also not so much to scare him away. "Okay, I'll go first. I don't like outdoorsy things."

This makes him laugh. "I'll keep that in mind. No outside dates."

"Well, not necessarily," I say. "There's a difference between outside and outdoors. Patio bars? Yes. Camping? No. Beaches? Yes. Hiking? Fuck no."

He laughs. "I never thought there was a difference."

"Oh, there is," I say. "I like to say it's the difference between outside-y and outdoorsy."

He lets that sit for a second. "That actually makes a ton of sense."

I smile, and gently bump his shoulder. "Okay, there's one of mine. What about you?"

He brings me in a little tighter. "I have a habit of communicating in memes."

"I don't consider that a red flag. To me that's almost a love language."

"I'll take that," he says. "And I do need to admit, up until recently, I used two-in-one shampoo."

I laugh under my breath, though I am glad he told me that

up front because now I know I can shower at his house. "Please tell me you have a bed frame."

"I do. But I don't have any pictures in my apartment. Not for any other reason than I never remember to take photos."

"Same," I say. "I'm the worst."

He smiles and digs his phone out of his pocket. "Well, then, we're going to have to remind each other to capture the moments."

He pulls me in, holding his phone up to get a selfie of the two of us. I'm leaned into his shoulder, head slightly tilted, and if anyone was walking by it would look like this is date one hundred, not number one.

Fuck, I really am screwed…

He puts the phone down, but neither of us move much. I can tell the night's coming to an end, but like before, I don't want it to. But the next step is to ask him to come back to my place, and I'm not going to be the one to bring that up. I won't say no if he does, but there's enough of Katherine still controlling the wheel to let me know I need to pump the brakes, at least until I know we're on the same page.

"I should tell you one more thing," he says, his words barely a whisper as his hand rubs aimlessly on my arm.

"What's that?"

"I don't share."

I sit up so I can look at him, because that one I wasn't ready for. "You don't share? Like food? Because that's a good one to tell me, because I steal french fries regularly."

He laughs, but shakes his head, as he brings me back in. "I guess the better way to say it is that I'm a pretty selfish bastard."

Oh. That is a red flag. "How so?"

If he brought me in any closer, I'd be on his lap. Which I wouldn't be mad about. Not in the least bit. "What I mean is, that when I'm with a woman, I want her all to myself. I don't like to share."

I know what he said earlier about cheating, but just hearing the slight growl to his voice, and the octave that it dropped, I have a feeling he's talking about more than monogamy. And while I agree with him, I still want to have some fun and rile him up.

"I heard sharing is caring."

Grayson's eyes heat at words. "I don't share, Kat, but not in the way you're thinking. What I mean is that when I make a woman scream, yes, it's for her. Every time. But it's for me, as well. Because there is nothing, and I mean *nothing*, sexier than watching a woman come apart because of me. So when I say I'm selfish, it's because I want it all for myself. Every last drop. Every scream. Every breath. Just for me."

Oh my…

I've heard of men like this. Though, I was beginning to think they were made up, like Santa Claus or Rudolph. He might've started this conversation about red flags, but if what he's saying is true, the only flag anyone will be waving is a white one in surrender.

His fingers are slowly tracing the side of my cheek before pushing back a lock of hair. "That sound good, Kat?"

I nod, doing my best to gather my words when all I want to do is become putty in his hands. "It does. But I need some clarification."

"Ask away."

"I'm going to assume from this conversation, that you're a giver," I say as I let my fingers start aimlessly tracing up and down his arm. "The problem is, so am I. How's that going to work? Because while sharing is caring, my love language is acts of service. And I really, *really*, love to serve."

I know he thought he had me with his comment about not sharing. And don't get me wrong, he absolutely did. But the way he's looking at me right now? Lust and heat and desire pooling in his hazel eyes? I think I might've just been crowned the champ.

"Kat…"

Our foreheads are now touching. I could move ever so slightly and I'd feel his lips on mine.

And I want to, but not yet. Because if I start now, I don't know if I'll be able to stop.

"Yes, Grayson?"

"Want to keep this night going?"

I love how this question has evolved over the night between us. I also love that we both know the answer.

"Your place or mine?"

guide to christmas (and love) rule #20

Every woman's Christmas list should include a six-foot man with perfect facial scruff who can make you…excited.

4

kat

The answer was neither place. The answer was a four-star hotel two blocks away, because the wait time for a ride share was more than twenty minutes, and frankly, that was just too long to wait.

"How did you do that?" Grayson asks as the hotel desk clerk hands me the only key we'll need for the night. "Did you even put down a credit card?"

I shake my head as I take his hand and lead him to the elevator. "Didn't need to."

He gives me a questioning look as we wait for the elevator to take us to the penthouse suite. "Do I want to know or will that make me some sort of accomplice?"

I laugh as I turn toward him, tugging him in a little closer by his ridiculous, yet somehow sexy, Christmas sweater. "Nothing we'll go to jail for. I'm just taking advantage of my boss being a big deal. He has a room here for whenever him and his wife want it. And since they had a Christmas concert tonight for their son, I doubt they'll be having date night after."

I can tell by the look in Grayson's eyes that he's trying to figure out who the hell my boss would be that he'd have access to a penthouse suite at his disposal. And since the last thing I want to do is talk about my billionaire boss/best friend any more than I already have tonight, I do what I know will take his mind off of it.

I kiss him.

There's one second of shock. Which I get. I know many women who aren't comfortable making the first move, especially in a hotel lobby with people walking past us. And this isn't even where I thought our first kiss would happen. It probably should've happened when we were eating our hot dogs on the bench. Or countless other times during our impromptu night. But this…it somehow feels right.

Grayson relaxes within a second and leans into the kiss. My God, does he lean into it. His hands move to the small of my back, pressing me into him so I can feel every inch of his hardening cock.

Yup, getting this hotel was exactly the right call.

Thank you, Logan.

My hands are itching to explore more of him, but I'm reminded that we're in a public place when the sound of the elevator arriving breaks our moment. We slowly move apart as the door opens, stepping aside to let out the other guests. But Grayson doesn't let me get too far from him, pulling me back against his hard chest as we wait to enter.

Finally we are thankfully alone.

"Come here," Grayson growls out, pulling me against him before the door even closes. Our feet stumble back, pinning me against the wall. Our tongues are searching for more as this kiss continues to deepen. Both of us want more. Both of us need more. And if not for someone entering at any moment, I'm pretty sure both of us would say fuck waiting for the room and start stripping each other right here.

The kiss has all the heat and passion of a crazy one-night stand. The desire. The franticness. The hands trying to cover as much ground as possible because you know your time together is limited.

But I hope they aren't. Tonight's connection with Grayson is something I haven't felt in…maybe ever. Even the only serious relationship I've had in my adult life didn't feel like this, and we were together for more than a year. Sure, the sex was good (mostly). We had fun (occasionally). But the instant spark that Grayson and I shared tonight is not anything I've felt before. So as much as I want this night—and to feel that beard against my skin in all the right places—I hope it's not the only time this happens.

Because I already can tell that I want more. I just hope he does as well.

Just as our hands are starting to roam in the places I've been aching to touch and be touched, the elevator comes to a stop, jolting us apart and opening to the penthouse suite.

Grayson pulls away just enough for me to start walking, but before I'm two steps out of the elevator, he pulls me back into him, my back to his front, before wrapping his arms around my stomach.

"You know I'm not going to run away," I say through a giggle as we talk in tandem to the door.

"I know," he says as his hands slide up my stomach, cupping my breasts. *How am I supposed to get a door open when this is happening?* "But if you ran, I couldn't do this."

All thoughts of a door, or really anything, fly out of my brain when Grayson's hands are on me. My head falls back onto his shoulder as teases me in the perfect places. Now, if he were to just start kissing my neck while he's doing this, I'd do anything he asked tonight.

Even that.

Yes, *that.*

"Are you going to let us in the room, Kat?" he asks, his lips dangerously close to *that* territory. "Or are you just going to let me tease you all night?"

I try my best to regain any brain function, but just as I do, he lightly nibbles on my neck, pinching my nipples through my sweater and bra. His fingers slowly start inching up my leather skirt sending shivers up my spine.

"Grayson..." His name spills out of my lips as I fail yet again to step closer to the door, and therefore let us in. "I need more."

"Then let us in the room, Kat," he murmurs in my ear. "The quicker we're inside, the quicker I can lick that sweet pussy that I know is wet and ready for me."

His words snap me out of my fog, my body instantly ready for every single word that just came out of his deliciously dirty mouth.

Because it is. It so is.

I hurry and insert the key card to the door, the green light flashing and allowing me to push in with ease. Grayson and I stumble into the room, and I barely have my feet under me before he spins me around and pins me against the wall.

Yes, a million times yes, is the only thing going through my head. The feel of his body pressed against mine, the hard wall behind me. His mouth claiming mine like it's his to do with what he wants.

One million, bajillion, infinity times yes.

Our hands are clawing at each other, both having the same idea as we start to lift up each other's sweaters. We break our kiss, both smiling through ragged breaths, when we realize we're about to get tangled. He lets go of mine, lifting his arms up over his head. Our eyes stay locked as run my fingers under his sweater, allowing my hands to explore while I push up the material over his head.

I'd felt his chest against me earlier. I felt it on the dance floor. I leaned into it while he was teasing me. But seeing it now...the definition in his muscles that isn't too bulky but it lets me know that the man definitely hits the gym...the dusting of chest hair that I know will feel delicious against my bare skin in just a matter of minutes...it's more than I could've imagined. I feel my mouth watering, and my mind is spiraling with the naughtiest of thoughts as he puts his arms down, tossing the garment to the side.

I unconsciously lick my lips as I reach for the bottom of my sweater to take it off. The heat is just too much to bear, between the woolen fabric and Grayson's gaze. But the second I start to move it up, he takes both of my hands in his, bringing them above my head, his pelvis pressing into me so I have nowhere to go.

"Oh no," he says in a low, deep voice. "This is my present. Don't you dare unwrap it."

In any other setting, and if it were any other man, I'd be cracking up right now over his horrible Christmas pun. But in this case, as I feel his hands slide up my side, pushing up the knitted fabric, and the immediate sensation of the cold air hitting my exposed skin, there's nothing to laugh about. Quite the contrary. I have nothing to say. There's nothing I *want* to say. The only thing I want to do with my mouth is kiss this man.

"Fuck, Kat," he says as he stares down at my chest. "I had a feeling I was going to get lost in these tonight. And I'm glad I was so fucking right."

A ping of regret hits me as it's only then that I realize I'm wearing the boring Katherine lingerie. The beige bra has lace on it, but the panties are full coverage and in no way sexy. Yet, I don't think Grayson gives two fucks. He doesn't even bother taking down the straps as he pushes both of my tits together before burying his face into the crease.

Now, being a bigger-chested woman, and having been with men who know and don't know what do in the bedroom, an act like this has only ever gone one of two ways. There's the disappointing way: The men who see a pair of breasts with a cup size bigger than "D" and lose all brain power. That also means they lose any—if they had any—sense of how to not just motorboat you into oblivion. Sure, they love it, but me? Not so much.

But then there are the men like Grayson. The ones whose touch is just as much for them as it is for me. Where there's massaging and squeezing, kissing and sucking, lapping and tasting. Every movement, every kiss, and every suck, is sending shivers through my body. And if I had any questions on whether or not this is turning him on, that's quickly answered by the feel of his hard cock grinding into me.

My breathing is picking up, and somehow I'm hotter now than I was a minute ago with my sweater on. As if he can read my mind, Grayson slides the straps down my shoulders before reaching behind and expertly unfastening my bra with two quick flicks of his fingers.

Skills like that are going to bode very well for later…

Grayson steps back, looking at me with reverence as I stand topless before him, my chest heaving, in nothing now but knee-high boots and a black leather skirt.

"Fucking gorgeous."

The low register of his voice hits me straight in the pussy. I feel it clench as his words echo off the walls surrounding us.

"I can say the same thing."

I step off the wall and take Grayson's hand in mine as I lead him down the hallway of the penthouse to the master bedroom. It's an expansive space with a California King and floor-to-ceiling windows. If you were to open the curtains, you'd have a gorgeous view of downtown Nashville. But I don't, because I have a much more up-close and personal view in mind.

I swing Grayson around, walking him back until he falls into the bed. I follow him down, my hands holding me up as they are on either side of him, needing to taste his lips one more time before they are otherwise occupied. He tries to bring me down, his hands finding my exposed breasts, but just as he's able to gently twist my nipple, I move back.

"You've had your fun," I say. "Now it's my turn."

I stand up, but just enough to allow me to unfasten his belt and bring down the zipper of his jeans. He doesn't say anything as I gather his boxer briefs as well, sliding them down his legs. Just as I have everything removed, I allow myself to look back up at him, and…holy fucking about-to-be-born baby Jesus…the man is huge.

Leave it to the redheads…they always bless you with a surprise.

I was ready for the length. I could feel that against me numerous times tonight. But what I wasn't prepared for was the sheer girth of this man. The combination should be illegal.

But hey, I'm always up for a challenge. And this is going to be a very, very satisfying one.

His hand grips his cock as I take a step back, stroking himself as I reach to the side to unzip the leather skirt I decided to wear tonight. I don't know why I did. It's not a very Katherine skirt. Maybe somehow, in my subconscious, I wanted to be Kat tonight as well. Whatever the reason, I'm glad I did. I feel sexy. And the way that Grayson's looking at me right now, as I'm turned to the side, bending over expertly as I push the skirt and panties off my hips, is a moment I'm never going to forget.

Nope. I'll be telling people at the nursing home about this.

Wanting to keep the show going, I bend down to reach for the zipper of my boots, but Grayson's voice pulls me away.

"No," he commands. I look back up, nervous for a second, but that's until I see the wicked smile on his face and his hand still stroking his cock. "Those stay on."

Oh, this is going to be fun.

"That can be arranged," I say as I step back toward him, lowering myself to my knees. "Though you won't be able to get the view of them *quite* yet."

He sees the glint in my eyes and moves his hand away, which I immediately replace as I take over working him from base to tip. He moans my name as I stroke up and down, loving the fact that I can barely get my fingers around him.

We keep our eyes on each other as I lower my head, my tongue coming out so I can start lightly licking around the tip. It only takes a few swirls before he throws his head back, and when I take him into my mouth, that's it—he collapses onto the bed, losing all ability to hold himself up.

"Fucking fuck," he growls out, his hands finding my hair. "Don't stop. Please don't ever fucking stop."

I smile a little as I continue to work him, because that reaction? To me? That's in the top-five departments of ways to turn Kat Smith on. Yes, foreplay from him—and a good fingering with a perfect execution of locating my G-Spot—are at the top. But giving a blow job? Knowing the power I feel when I can bring a man to his knees—or like now when Grayson is moaning nonsense and unable to hold himself up—that will get me going every fucking time.

I release him for a second, needing to swallow and stretch out my jaw, which gives him the moment to sit back up.

"Okay so far?" I ask as our eyes lock.

"Okay doesn't even begin to describe it."

I notice that his eyes are on line, but I can see the heat in them as he stares at my chest.

Oh, now there's an idea.

"Keep your eyes on me..."

He does as I ask, his breathing picking up as I crawl onto the bed with him. He moans out something inaudible the second that I let my tongue drift over his cock, licking it like it's the best lollipop in the world.

"Fuck me," Grayson moans. I could stay down here all day, but this act is just a means to an end. Because just as he thinks I'm settling in, I slowly stop and crawl closer to him, placing each of my tits around his cock.

"Squeeze them together," I tell him. "Then I'll do the rest."

Blazing. That's the only thing I see in his hazel eyes as I move up and down on him as his cock fucks my tits.

"Goddamn, Kat," he says through a ragged breath. "So fucking amazing."

Our eyes stay locked as I continue to work him, which seems somehow more intimate than what I'm doing to him right now. Eye contact is usually awkward. Me saying things like "eyes on me" is not something in my repertoire. But with Grayson? Not only do I not want to break this stare, it's almost if I can't. He has a hold on me. I couldn't look away if I tried.

"Come here," he says, letting go of my tits as he rolls me over to my back. "Didn't you say sharing is caring?"

I smile as he moves my hands over my head. "I believe I did."

"Well, then, it's my turn."

He places one more rough kiss on my lips before he begins moving his lips down my body. If he wants to set up camp at my chest, he resists the temptation—though he does suck on each nipple once for good measure—before he moves to my center.

"Fuck yes," I say as I relax into the bed, my legs widening as Grayson kisses around my center before making his way to where I need him the most.

Holy…shit…

My mind is going blank as his tongue starts swirling around, hitting every nerve ending with exactly the right pressure. If the headboard had bars, I'd be grabbing them right now, but instead I let my hands come down, holding onto his hair as he further buries himself into me.

I haven't written to Santa Claus in years—ever since I was eight and I asked him for concert tickets and he brought me a karaoke machine instead—but I think, somehow, someone slipped him a note from me. That's the only way I can think that I was gifted a man who is my kind of hot, isn't afraid to wear a ridiculous Christmas sweater, has a dick that could literally wreck a person, and can eat pussy like it's his last meal and he's refusing to let a drop go to waste.

Yup. Santa is real, and I'm once again a believer.

I start to get lost in the feel of Grayson's mouth when he adds two fingers. My back arches as he works them in me, searching for just the right spot as his tongue rapidly flicks on my clit. I was just holding onto his hair before, but now I'm about to pull it out of his head. Because between his tongue—holy mother of Jesus, his tongue—and his fingers… It's too… I can't…

"Fuck!"

The word is followed by a few more sounds that are unintelligible. I'm not sure. I'm also not sure what is happening to my body, because it's shaking. Something may have exploded. All I'm sure of is that the high I just felt is like nothing I've ever experienced before.

And if this is just one night, then I'm going to remember it forever.

But I'm hoping it's not.

"Fucking hell," I wheeze breathlessly as Grayson moves to lay next to me. "That was…"

"Just the beginning," he says with a smile before rolling me on top of him. "We're just getting started."

5

grayson

Unpopular opinion in the male demographic: I love waking up with a woman in my arms.

Especially right now and this woman.

I don't know what it is. The feeling of her soft skin on my chest? The warmness from her body? The way her leg is casually slung over my body, like she's trying to wrap herself around me like a spider monkey? It doesn't get any better than this.

Well, it could. But I don't know if I have it in me. I've never in my life turned down morning sex—it's in the top three of all sexes—but after our marathon last night, I don't know if either of us have it in us.

But if she wanted to, I guess I'd find the strength…

I feel her start to move on me as I turn to look at the clock. It's seven in the morning, and I'm thanking the corporate business world gods that my bosses told me I could come in late today since I was technically working last night.

Best night of work ever!

"What time is it?" she mumbles into my chest.

"Just after seven."

She's quiet again, slowly stretching her arms and legs, all while staying close to me. "Do you have to go to work?"

"Not for a bit," I say as I place a kiss on her forehead.

"Well that's good," she says as she rolls on top of me. "Because I'm not ready to say goodbye."

Kat's lips press down into mine in what I can only describe as the laziest, yet deepest, kiss we've shared in the crazy twelve hours that we've known each other. There's nothing desperate in this. No, this is just two people, whose mouths are now intimately familiar with each other, sharing a moment. Sharing a connection.

One that I'm not ready to let go of just yet.

Neither of us said anything last night about where this might go, or if it's going to be lived in my memory as the hottest night of my life with a woman who I'm pretty sure has ruined me for others. I mean, she was at a speed-dating event, so I'm assuming she's looking for more than a casual relationship. And yes, I was there to impress Hazel, but I wasn't against possibly meeting someone. Sure, this morning doubt could've been saved by a simple conversation last night. But I had much more important things on my mind than having the "so what is this" chat.

Much, much more important things. Things that I'd like to repeat. Multiple times.

My dick starts to grow hard as our kiss continues, our weight shifting us to our sides. Kat repositions herself around my thigh, but at the same time, pulls away from my lips.

"Can I be a mood killer?"

I quirk my eyebrow as her eyes shift down, then back up to mine. "Depends…"

Her smile is bashful, and one I haven't seen before. "While the idea of another round sounds great in theory, I don't know if I can."

I smile before I lean back in, kissing her one more time. "Not a mood killer. If anything, that makes my mood very good."

"I'm sure it does," she says as she pulls herself even closer to me. "Last night was…"

I tap my forehead to hers, because I don't have words for it either. "Yes, it was."

We lie there in silence for more than a few minutes, our fingers trailing aimlessly on each other's skin. I know the clock is ticking, and eventually I need to leave this bed, but I'm not ready. At least, not before I know I can see her again.

"Can I call you? Take you out on a proper first date that isn't hot dogs?"

She doesn't say anything for a second, and dread begins to creep in. Every bad thought goes through my head before I see the smile I'm learning to look for.

"I'd like that."

Relief washes through me as I lean down and kiss her forehead. "Then it's a date."

I seal it with a kiss on her lips before she quickly pulls away and makes a face. "Shit—don't be mad at me."

"Kat. Unless you're going to tell me you're married, or worse, a dating a professional hockey player who could kick my ass, I don't see how I could be mad at you."

That makes her laugh. "It's nothing like that. It's just that I have to go out of town for work this weekend. Plus, I know the holidays are coming up, which always makes things weird. I just…if I can't meet with you right away, I hope you don't think it's because I'm not interested. Because I am."

I roll her over, giving me another look into her brown eyes. The ones I got lost in too many times last night. The ones I know I'm going to get lost in many times over in the future.

Because yes, I see a future with this woman. I wasn't lying last night when I told her that if I didn't see a relationship going somewhere, I was quick to cut it. If I didn't feel anything this morning, I would've treated this like a one-night stand. Neither are true. I want to see where this goes, which I hope is far.

"If you think because of some scheduling issues that I'm going to lose interest, then I don't think you realize how determined and stubborn I can be."

This makes her smile again as she starts playing with the hair at the nape of my neck. "Well, that's good. But so am I. How do you think this is going to work?"

I lean down, my cock that's been semi-hard all morning now fully erect as it rubs against her. "I'm not sure. But I'm sure we'll figure out a way."

Kat's hand moves down between us, slowly stroking me. "I think we can. And I think we should start now."

I roll her on top of me, her giggles filling the room as we become tangled in each other one more time. "I thought you were a mood killer?"

She shakes her head and adds a devilish smile. "My moods change often. You ready for that?"

I pull her closer to me, our lips inches away. "I'm ready for it all."

———

On any given Friday, most people in an office are smiling—especially when it's the Friday before your company is giving you the last two weeks of the year off for the holidays. The only thing on the office's agenda is our holiday party, featuring a massive dessert table, catered lunch, and our white elephant gift exchange, or as they apparently call it in the south, Dirty Santa.

If that was the only thing on the agenda today, I'd still be smiling like the kid who got exactly what he wanted for Christmas. But considering I still have the vivid memory of Kat's naked body lying on top of me, and the shower we took together this morning before leaving the hotel room, this smile is here for the long haul.

"He's arrived." I look up from my desk to see my boss, Melinda, walking into my office. "How'd last night go?"

I know she's asking me about the speed dating event, and if it swayed Hazel in our direction. But the aforementioned smile plastered on my face likely gives away that I'm grinning about a lot more than an account.

"It went really well." And it did. No lies there. "Was a really good event. I think we could do some great things with their company."

"I'm just happy you got in the door," she says as she takes a seat across from me. "Hazel has kept everything in house for years. The fact that she's venturing out was an opportunity I'm glad we could take advantage of."

"Absolutely," I say as I flick on my computer. "She didn't give me a timetable for when she's making her decision. I'm going to guess, if she's like most other companies, I'm not going to hear back until after the first of the year."

"Good to know if anyone asks," Melinda says. "Now you can take the rest of the year off and come back ready to work hard in January."

I shake my head. "Nope. What's next?"

Melinda narrows her eyes at me, giving me a stern mom stare. Which I guess fits. Her son is older than me, and I've seen her go off on some interns who didn't follow directions.

"Grayson, it's the Friday before a two-week vacation. Look out into the bullpen. Not a single person in this office is working today. I'm barely working. Why not fall into peer pressure and slack off today, instead of asking me who the next whale is that you're trying to bag?"

"What can I say? The work never stops."

"It does. And you need it to," she says. "I can't afford for you to burn out. You're my best publicist. I need you to take it easy these next two weeks."

She's probably right, though I hate admitting it out loud. I've been going nonstop all year. The smart thing for my mental and physical health should be unwinding and resting. Binging a show. Going home to visit my family for a few days. Maybe sneaking in a few dates with Kat when she's back in town.

But the thought of completely pumping the brakes right now

isn't going to happen. I won't work all the time. But between the binging and the eating and the dating, I'm going to be doing my research. Making my game plans. Because next year is going to be the year that I climb the ladder and finally have the title of Senior Account Executive.

When I get the promotion—because it's not if, but when—I'll be the youngest senior account executive, at the ripe old age of thirty-four. And while it's not completely unheard of for somebody my age to get promoted to that level, it would be a first for Sterling Strategies.

And that's what I want to be. The first. The best. Anything less is unacceptable. If I'm going to be the black sheep of my family by not following in the footsteps of the family business, then being the best is my only option.

I remember the day that I knew that being at the top of my field was going to be the only way to earn my family's approval. It was the moment I told them I was going to Boston University for public relations and not to Cornell for law, like every member of my family has done for the past three generations. I remember the shocked gasps and dropped jaws. Because how dare I not follow in the Ross family footsteps and join the law practice of Ross and Family Associates—a law firm that has been in my family for seventy-three years and used to be named Ross and Sons but had to change when my sister became the first female lawyer in our family. Along with my sister, my younger brother is also a lawyer. So are all eleven of my cousins. Obviously, their fathers, along with mine, were lawyers. And my grandfather.

Then there's me. The outcast. The ne'er-do-well. The only one to move outside of Connecticut to do what he wanted to do, despite being the oldest of this generation of Rosses.

To say that my family doesn't get my life choices is a drastic understatement. Which is why I only plan on spending forty-eight hours with them over the holidays. I learned a few years ago two days was the sweet spot. A person can only be on the receiving ends of tsks and condescending looks for so long.

Yup, I'm the family failure in every sense of the word. They don't see the success I've had. They didn't understand why I opted to spend my summers in college interning in Boston or New York. Why I studied so hard.

Maybe one day they will. But until then, all I can do is keep grinding.

"Really, Melinda? There's nothing?" I ask again. "Not even the sniff of a lead?"

She shakes her head. "Sorry, Grayson. It's the end of the year, so the well is pretty dry. There are some smaller inquiries and accounts we have an eye on, but I was going to toss those to the juniors."

I nod and sit back in my seat. While I have a drive to be the best, I also know what my time is best spent on. Plus, I remember my days starting out and salivating at every possible account or project I'd get fed. I wanted to make it the best. Show my bosses what I could do. I wouldn't be here today if I didn't have those early experiences, and I'd never want to take that away from someone getting started.

It's now confirmed: My Christmas break will be spent researching the whales. Or, maybe doing some digging on the one person in this town who's keeping me from them: fucking Katherine Smith.

Seriously, who is she and what's she doing that's so much better than what I'm bringing to the table? If I can figure that out, it'll be better than any Christmas present.

"How about a beach?" Melinda asks. "I think you could do well with a beach. I recommend St. Lucia. To me, you can't go wrong there."

My first instinct is to dismiss her idea, but frankly, a beach sounds kind of nice right now. Warm weather. A drink with an umbrella. Beautiful women. Though after last night, the only beautiful woman I want to see in a bikini is Kat.

Oh, Kat on a beach… Now there's an idea.

As my brain starts to wander off to the image of Kat with

sun-kissed skin, the telltale sound of an email pings through. The Pavlovian response I have to it immediately has me navigating to the browser to see who it's from, and when I see the name I immediately suck in a breath.

"What is it?" Melinda asks.

I take a few deep breaths to calm myself. "It's Hazel."

"Fuck."

I don't have to open the email to know what it's going to say. It's going to be a rejection letter. That's why you get an email. Phone calls mean you get it. Emails means you didn't.

Grayson,

I want to start off by saying thank you very much for presenting your ideas to Left for Love and Quiz and Cupid. Your ideas were fresh, bright, and exactly on line with what we were looking for. Unfortunately, though, we will be going a different direction with our campaign's public relation and media strategy needs. Again, thank you for your ideas, and I really hope we can work together in the future.
Happy holidays,
Hazel Montgomery-Calhoun

I fall back into my chair and close my eyes, trying to breathe through the anger I'm feeling right now.

"She fucking did it again," I say under my breath.

"Who's she?" Melinda asks.

Okay, apparently it wasn't as under my breath as I thought. "Katherine fucking Smith."

Do I know for a fact she's the one who Hazel's going with? No. But I know what my track record was *before* she came to town, and I know after. And because I'm a betting man, I'm going all-in on the fact that somehow this woman has bested me again.

"She's some new fucking independent media specialist. And I have it on good authority that she's the one I've lost out to in the last three pitches I've made."

I'd expect my boss to have my back on this one, be just as mad as I am, but instead, she just has an amused smile on her face.

"Sounds like my kind of girl. We should hire her."

"You're not helping, and fuck no," I say, horrified, which only makes Melinda laugh. "This isn't funny."

"Oh, but it is."

"Care to tell me how?"

"Because, this woman is going to make you better."

I'm a little thrown by her words. "And how is that?"

Melinda stands up, but doesn't make her way to the door quite yet. "We all have our rivals when we're coming up in this industry. Some are in-house, some are competitors. Does it suck losing to them? Absolutely. But you do one of two things: You can pout that you lost and act like a toddler, or you can use it to make yourself better. Because at the end of the day, that's all a rival does, is make you better. If you let her."

I don't respond, but let her words sit, because she's right—though I am going to pout for just a minute. But after I'm done pouting, I refocus on what my Christmas plan was. Yes, I'm going to figure out who Katherine Smith is. I'm going to figure out her pitches. What she's doing. How she does it. What she's doing that I'm not.

Because she's not going to get the best of me forever. And today's win was the last one she's going to have.

"Timberline Inn."

I'm very confused, because I've never heard that name before. "Excuse me?"

"Timberline Inn. That's what you can work on over Christmas break. Get your mojo back. Start the new year off with a bang. The owner, Howard, has worked with us for years and was asking if we had anyone available for a project starting after the first of the year. How about you go up there for a few days, clear your head with that Smoky Mountain air, and then meet with him next week before you take off for the holidays?"

That…sounds absolutely perfect. "Thank you."

Melinda gives me a warm smile. "Anytime."

She starts to walk away, but there's one other thing I need to ask her. "Melinda. You said you had a rival. How did it end?"

She cracks a smile. "I married him."

With those words, Melinda turns to leave my office, and she's not even two steps out the door before I am searching up the Timberline Inn.

It's an old hotel in East Tennessee, right in the heart of the Smoky Mountains. It's giving a lodge and cabin vibe, but without actually being in a cabin. There seems to be a nice-looking restaurant, a decent bar, and plenty of activities that guests can register to do. And look at that, they have a room open for the next few days.

Yes, this is exactly what I need. A new client. A few days away to regroup and actually relax before I go to see my family. And far enough away that Katherine Smith isn't going to be anywhere near me.

guide to christmas (and love) rule #79

A true friend always knows what you want for Christmas. And when you've hooked up.

6
kat

"ARE CONGRATULATIONS IN ORDER?"

I look up from my desk at the newly built headquarters of GameTech, to see my best friend and occasional boss, Logan Matthews, leaning against my doorframe, a cautious look of hopefulness on his face.

"That would be a yes," I say, unable to keep the smile off mine. I feel like that's all I've been doing today. Then again, when you start your day with an orgasm, it's hard not to smile like a fool. Add in the phone call I just got from Hazel, and that means this smile isn't coming off my face for a long, long time.

"She loved my ideas and thinks I'm going to bring a completely different approach to their media campaign than they envisioned, but one they are very excited about. Once the holidays are over, she wants us to schedule a meeting to officially get things going."

"Bravo," Logan says, his British accent coming through. "Though, was it even a question that you'd get it?"

"I mean, it always is," I say plainly. "The day that I assume I'm going to get every client is the day I need to take a hard look in the mirror. Nothing's guaranteed."

That's the public relations statement coming out in me.

Logan's eyebrow goes up, knowing me too well for my practiced speech. "But since you've started seeking work outside of GameTech, haven't you gotten every one you've tried for?"

I give a nonchalant shrug. "I mean, technically yes. But who's counting?"

We share a laugh as Logan takes a seat at one of the chairs on the other side of my desk. "Can you believe us?"

"In what way?"

He holds his hands up and looks around the glass-walled office he made sure I had when he officially moved GameTech's operations from the West Coast to Nashville. "This. Everything. SpaceCraft is on top of the world again. We're expanding our game brands. You have this place running so smoothly you can go back to chasing clients like you used to, but on your terms. We're doing everything we ever wanted to do."

We really are. When Logan and I met in college, we were both wide-eyed, eighteen-year-olds with big dreams. He wanted to develop a video game that entertained the masses, and I wanted to be one of the best corporate publicists in the business.

It wasn't an easy road to get here. The first office we had was our kitchen table, which we found at a yard sale for seven bucks. We had two mismatched chairs, but it's where we sat every night as he talked about his game and I busted my ass trying to climb the ladder at my first corporate PR job.

I shiver just thinking about that place.

When I was in college, people in my major all wanted to be celebrity publicists. Live in Los Angeles. Work for A-list clients. Yes, you get invited to glamorous parties, but in exchange you spend most of your time making sure your clients don't end up on Page Six for some sort of nefarious thing.

Frankly, that sounds exhausting.

Which is why I picked the area that I've excelled in—corporate PR. Working with million- and billion-dollar companies to cultivate a new product launch, or to completely shift the identity of the business to make them profitable? Now that's my jam.

When SpaceCraft exploded onto the scene, and Logan formed the GameTech corporation, I was his first hire as head of media strategies. Not only did he pull me from a horrible situation with my former job, but he gave me the freedom to be the best version of my corporate self. I went from hating going to work every day to working for my best friend while helping him take his video game from a dream in our kitchen to a billion-dollar industry.

That's why I got into this business, and that's why I wanted to branch out. Knowing that I, as one woman, single handedly have done a job that companies sometimes hire an entire team to do? Now that's a fucking power trip I'll get off on any day.

It's like giving a corporate blow job.

And of course now that I'm thinking of blow jobs, I'm thinking of Grayson, and the smile is right back on my face. I know I told him I couldn't see him for a few days, but I'm technically free tonight. I wonder if he'd like another go round before we have to say our holiday goodbyes…

"Well, congratulations again," Logan says. But just as he's about to stand up, he sits right back down. "Oh, and I meant to ask you…any idea why my credit card was charged last night at the Omni Hotel? Did I stay there last night and forget about it?"

I've never had a great poker face, but even if I did, I don't think I could hide my reaction. If it was anyone else, I'd do my best to deflect and gaslight a bit—also known as Public Relations 101. But because this is Logan, and there's not a person on this planet who knows me better, I fess up. It's really just easier.

"I might've used your room last night."

"Might've? How might you have used it? Please Kat, I'd love to hear how one 'might' use a room?"

The Joker-esque grin on his face means he's catching onto the smile that's been on mine since the moment he walked in. I know he's fucking with me, baiting me a bit, but I'm going to let him have it. I don't date often enough for him to give me shit, and God knows I gave him plenty when he was pining for his now wife.

"I might've met someone at the speed dating event I went to. And things might've went very well."

Why is my best friend's face lighting up like the Christmas tree we currently have in our lobby?

"Kat! That's amazing! Oh my God, we can double date!"

"Simmer down, Sparky," I say, because the man really does look like he's just opened his favorite Christmas present. "Yes, we had a very nice time last night. And yes, we spent the night together. We both expressed interest in seeing each other again after the holidays. But that's a long time away, so let's temper our excitement, okay?"

At least, that's what I'm trying to do. Sure, I've been smiling from ear to ear today, but there's the little voice on my shoulder that's warning me not to get too far ahead of myself. At the end of the day, I'm a realist, and I need to remember that. Because sure, we had a great night, and an even better morning. We exchanged numbers and shared a long kiss when we said good-bye. But two weeks is a long time, and the holidays can make those weeks feel like months. Minds could change. Things could happen. So until that time comes, I'm going remain cautiously optimistic, with an emphasis on the cautiously.

"Well now I feel bad," Logan says. "You're traveling over the holidays because of me. Do you want me to call Declan at the Timberline Inn and tell him you can't come?"

I shake my head. "Don't you even dare. If Grayson can't handle that sometimes my career comes first, it's better for me to know that now rather than later. Plus, he's traveling to visit his family. And I was looking for a few days of R&R. I booked myself a room for the weekend at the Timberline before my meeting with him on Monday. There's a nearby spa that looks delightful, and I might even roast a marshmallow or two."

Logan apparently doesn't care about my itinerary, instead deciding to focus on the first part of what I said.

"Grayson? I get to know his name? Usually when you start seeing someone, I'm only given a random nickname."

I laugh because he's right. "You love my nicknames."

"I really do," he says. "That's probably the saddest part of you not dating since we've been in Nashville. I mean, hearing about men like Captain Sweatpants? The Lip Biter? Or maybe my favorite, Johnny Talks Alot? Now those were the days."

I roll my eyes at that. I'm just glad that he didn't bring up The Cheat. "Talks Alot was the last date I went on in Los Angeles almost two years ago, and somewhere, if you listen really hard, he's now moved on to a presentation about why Blackberries are going to make a comeback."

Logan laughs as he reaches into his suit jacket. "Well, I'm sorry again that you're doing me this favor. And I hope that these can make up for it."

I take the envelope from him. "What's this?"

Logan gives me a warm smile. "Merry Christmas, Katherine."

I can barely believe my eyes when he pulls out an airplane ticket, along with a card that says words I have to read a few times to make sure I'm seeing right.

"Logan! A one-week, all-inclusive vacation in St. Lucia? Why? No. This is too much."

He shakes his head and holds up his hand as I try to give the envelope back to him. "Frankly it's not enough."

"Is this my Christmas gift? Because if so, then I drastically underspent." And here I was thinking that I knocked it out of the park when I found a collection of vintage video game posters. "Why did you do this?"

"Because I can," he says. "Partly because you're doing me this favor by going to Timberline. Declan's a nice guy, and he wants to do right by his hotel. Been in his family for a few generations. I know this isn't the kind of client you usually take on, but you going out there means the world to me."

"Is he talking to anyone else?"

Logan shakes his head. "I didn't get that impression, but I didn't ask, either."

"No worries." It was really just for my edification. Whether they are or not, I'm still going to give them the same level of presentation. "But Logan, going out to the Timberline Inn doesn't warrant an extravagant trip."

"It's not just that," he says, leaning over and grabbing my hands. "The gift was happening no matter what, because you deserve it. You got my life and my company on track. You helped me navigate the toughest year of my life. You've been my best mate for more than ten years. And I know that I'm not here without you. This ticket, this vacation, is just a small thing I can do to say thank you. For everything."

I don't cry often, but dammit, he's going to make me sniffly.

"I really don't have words," I say as I stand up and walk around the desk. "Thank you. For everything."

He stands up, and we share a hug. I know a lot of times he'll thank me for helping him navigate his business waters, and helping get SpaceCraft and GameTech to where they are today. But I owe this man everything. If it weren't for him, I'd be still working, and frankly, hating, my job in the corporate hustle and bustle. Now he's given me the job of my dreams and is allowing me the space to keep growing my business as well. He's supported me every step of the way.

I don't know what luck was cast upon me the day we met— two awkward freshmen standing next to each other at orientation—but I'll forever be eternally grateful for that day.

"You're welcome," he says as we pull away. "Now, please go enjoy yourself."

"I'll try," I say sarcastically. "Three days at a quaint, rustic, hotel followed by seven days in paradise? How will I ever manage?"

7

grayson

There's something to be said about a leisurely drive. I remember my grandpa doing it when I was young and was always confused about why he was driving just to drive. Once I asked him where he went, and I was baffled by his answer: he said he went to three states just that day to see the sights and picked up some syrup because he passed a road-side stand. Granted, we lived in New England, which made all of that possible. But still. I didn't get it.

Then I became an adult and realized how relaxing it could be just to hit the road. Yes, I'm on my way to the mountains for work, but this three-hour drive has been just about me, the road, the podcast I found that goes further in depth to some of the greatest sports stories of all time, and my car snacks.

Yes, there are snacks that are only allowed for road trips. And Nerd Clusters are those snacks.

Oh, and thinking a time or two about Kat. Okay, more than two. The woman has altered my psyche in some way. It hasn't even been two days since I last saw her, but I can't get her out of my head. Our text exchange from earlier doesn't help that.

GRAYSON

Hope you have a good trip. Safe travels today.

KAT

Thanks. Not on the road yet. Packing to be gone for multiple days is never easy.

Understandable. Probably one of those things guys have easier than women.

Yes. Because we have to do panty math.

Panty math?

Yes. It's the precise calculation of how many pairs to take, multiplied by the days there, divided by what type we need. And for the ten days I'll be gone, my total needs to be no less than twenty-five, but now I have to divide those up by style.

Ten days and twenty-five pairs? I hate to get personal, but do you plan on shitting yourself every day you're there?

Look, you never know. I never have, but you have to be prepared for anything.

I...I had no idea.

And I haven't even told you about the math of deciding what cut and style of underwear to bring. You have to have some for comfort, some for certain kinds of dresses, the list goes on.

Dresses, you say? What kind are we talking? I'm a big fan (especially the vision of you in one).

All different styles. Mostly the kind I have a feeling you'd rather see on the floor 😏

You're killing me, woman.

I'll make sure to send you a picture whenever I
wear one.

Is that my Christmas present?

Oh no. That will come after the new year. But
the dress (and the underwear) will be involved.

Yup, you're going to be the death of me.

But what a way to go, am I right?

She is right. But as much as I'd love to think about her and
her underwear, right now, my GPS signals that I'm about five
miles away from the Timberline Inn. Meaning it's time to focus.
Game plan. End my year with a win.

When I emailed the owner, Howard, yesterday, he got back to
me immediately and couldn't wait to meet me. He said that he
and his son were excited for the opportunity to sit down and
chat before the new year. However, he explained that he was
going to be gone all weekend, so he hoped it would be okay if
we meet Monday. Which is fine by me. That gives me a few days
to scope out the hotel, restaurant, bar, really anything I can get a
feel for, before putting together my pitch to him. The more I feel
like I know the product, the more I'm going to be able to wow
him. And if all goes well, I'll be on my plane to Connecticut on
Tuesday with a final win in the column to close out the year.

The one thing he was vague about was specifically what he
wanted a media strategy about. But as I pull up, I'm sure it can't
be the exterior, or even the overall building. It's a good-sized
hotel—I'd guess about two hundred rooms. But it's the facade
that's blowing me away. The combination of brick and wood
gives it a rustic feel. Add on the expertly placed Christmas lights
and lit garlands and it's the perfect holiday getaway. That's not
even mentioning the thirty-foot Christmas tree lit up in the
center of the grounds, which is the first thing you see when you
pull up.

Yeah…I'm going to be able to work with this. It's also the perfect place to kick off my holiday vacation.

I'm only more confident in this thought as I walk into the lobby. I know it's called an inn, but from the second you step inside, it's like you're transported to a ski lodge in Aspen, with the wood, the warmth, the fireplaces, and soft lighting. It's gorgeous. This is the absolutely perfect place to spend the holidays, or really, any time of the year. Families. Couples looking for getaways. Every place I look, something else catches my eye. It's why I'm not paying attention to my surroundings, and why I feel myself running into someone from behind.

"Oh my God, I'm so sor—" I turn around to apologize but the words can't leave my mouth. "Kat?"

I drop my backpack. My mouth is hanging open. Shocked doesn't even begin to describe my reaction. And judging by Kat's brown eyes also popping out of her head, she's just as surprised to see me.

"Grayson? What are you doing here? I thought you were going to Connecticut?"

I can't stop blinking, like at some point it's going to help, because this isn't happening. "Pitstop for work before I head up north. What about you? I thought you also had a business trip?"

"I am. This is where I'm staying."

I let out a laugh, because what are the fucking odds? I mean, this part of Tennessee isn't exactly desolate. The Smokys bring in a ton of tourism revenue with both chain and locally owned businesses, but still, the odds of us being here, at the same place at the same time, are staggeringly low.

"Okay, let's start this again," I say as I open my arms and take a deep breath. "Hey, you."

Her smile eases the awkwardness of the situation as she steps into my hold. "Hey, you."

We stand there for a few minutes, and I know I said this weekend was all business, but I can't help but now think that a little pleasure might be woven in.

"Have you checked in yet?" I ask as we step back from each other.

"No. Just pulled in a few minutes ago."

"Well, then, let's do it," I say as I pick up my bag, and being the gentleman I am, grab onto her suitcase and roll it to the check-in desk. "This is a pretty big suitcase. All of this, and all that panty math, for a trip to the mountains? Isn't that pretty outdoorsy?"

She laughs at my joke, and if I'm not mistaken the tiniest bit of a blush creeps on her cheeks. "No. After I'm done here, I'm on my way to St. Lucia. Christmas on a beach. What could be better?"

I laugh because, again, what are the odds? "My boss just told me that I should take a beach vacation and actually recommended I go there."

"I'll make sure to let you know how it is. In case you'd want to go there in the future."

"Please do."

We share a look that screams "we're about to see each other naked again really soon," when the front desk attendant calls up the next guest.

"Welcome to the Timberline Inn," she says cheerfully while also dawning reindeer ears. "Are the two of you checking in?"

We share a smile before Kat shakes her head. "No. We just happen to know each other. We're single reservations."

She's right. But if I have my way, neither of us are sleeping alone until we have to go our separate ways.

"Wonderful." The attendant asks for Kat's ID and credit card, and as she's doing that, something in the distance catches my attention.

"I'll be right back," I say, leaving my bags next to Kat as I make my way to the area so expansive that even calling it a "great room" feels like an injustice. Every space I walk into is more impressive than the last. Here there's a massive Christmas tree that takes up every vertical inch from floor to raised ceiling.

The soft, white lights give the room a certain glow that you can only get at Christmastime.

But what got my attention was the tinkling of a piano. I'd hoped as I walked in that it was somebody actually playing and not just piped-in sound, or worse, one of those auto-play ones. But no, there's a man, probably in his fifties, smiling away as he plays a Christmas carol on a grand piano. There are kids dancing and singing around him, as well as adults just sitting and taking in the atmosphere. And then there's me out of habit, moving my fingers against the air as if I'm the one pressing the keys.

It's been a while since I've played. A year? The last time I was in Connecticut? It had to have been. Maybe if I can sweet talk Howard, he'll let me tickle the ivories before I head off.

"Perfect timing," the attendant says as I walk back to the desk. "Name, please?"

"Grayson Ross," I say pulling out my credit card and license. "I booked yesterday."

"Great." She starts to type away, but with every click and clack of the keyboard, I watch her face get more and more worried.

"Mr. Ross?" She swallows hard before continuing. "I'm so very sorry about this."

"Sorry about what?"

She takes a breath and squares her shoulders, likely preparing for me to freak out for whatever she's about to say. "I need to start by explaining that our hotel has been going through renovations for the past year and a half. Through that time, we've closed off different areas so we can keep some capacity while also making the changes that our owner has wanted to implement."

"Sounds like smart business to me."

"Well, usually, yes. Unfortunately something must have glitched in the system, because the room that you're staying in is still under renovation and not available."

"Oh." The way she was freaking out, I was expecting a lot

worse. "That's no trouble. I just booked the first one that came up. Whatever room you have is fine with me."

"That's the next problem," she says, her eyes getting more scared. "There are no rooms available."

"Oh," I say, now understanding her impending panic. "Okay then. I can try and find—"

"Stay with me."

I look over to Kat, because while the thought did cross my mind, I didn't want to push her into something she might not be comfortable with.

"Are you sure?"

She flashes me a familiar smile—the one that looks awfully familiar to the night we met when she suggested we take our night to another location. "I'm sure. Plus, not like we haven't done this before." She quickly glances to the attendant, who hasn't taken a breath yet, before glancing back to me. "You know…share a room."

Oh this vixen…

"Okay, then, it's settled," I say and turn back to the very relieved-looking hotel worker. "Can we get a second key please?"

"Yes, absolutely," the attendant says and walks away. I take the break to turn back to Kat, needing to make sure one more time she's okay with this.

"Are you absolutely sure?" I ask. "I can find somewhere else to stay."

She shakes her head and leans into me. "I mean, I'd hoped that we'd be spending most nights together anyway. This just saves us the decision of whose room to go to."

I turn slightly to kiss her cheek, but don't pull away. "I love how your brain works."

"Work smarter, not harder. Am I right?"

"Right," I say, my voice coming out as a near growl as I grab our bags. "So fucking right."

———

I have no less than a thousand questions to ask Kat. How did it never come up that we'd both be in East Tennessee? What kind of work does she do that also brings her here? And how in all the hotels in all of Rocky Top did we both end up here? Together?

But I'll have plenty of time to ask all of those and more. Right now the only thing on my mind is kissing the hell out of this woman. I wanted to in the elevator. So did she. I could see it. Instead, we shared knowing looks about what happened the last time we were in an elevator, and what's going to happen the second we're inside our room.

"Door. Now." I say into her ear, knowing I'm not helping one bit as I kiss down her neck as she tries to insert the key card.

"It's not working," she says, though I'm not sure how much she's really trying. I seem to have found the spot on her neck where just a breath makes her literally melt into my arms.

"Do you want me to try?"

She nods and hands me the key. I step around her to get a better angle, but Kat doesn't move. She stays right next to me, her hand not so slyly rubbing over my cock, and she presses those tits that I haven't been able to get out of my mind into my arm.

"Kat…" I groan as I try to insert the card.

"What? Am I distracting you?"

"You know you are," I say as I pull the card out too quickly, flashing the red light.

"I'm just saying, it's not as easy as it looks."

Her hand wraps around my cock through my jeans, squeezing it just enough to send the perfect amount of pleasure through me. Knowing I can't wait a second more, I concentrate harder on this than I've concentrated on anything in my life, insert the key, and by the grace of the hotel gods it opens up.

We barely have our bags inside and the door hasn't even latched before our lips are crashing together. We're kissing like we haven't seen each other in months, not just days. Our hands are everywhere, as lips are begging, and our feet are stumbling backward, hopefully leading us to a bed.

Shirts are already coming off as Kat and I literally fall into the mattress that somehow we found. We calm slightly and my weight settles in on top of her as our mouths and hands start to rediscover each other. Her legs are wrapping around me as I move down the cup of her bra—navy this time—as my mouth lowers to her nipple.

I feel her body squirm under me as I start kissing and sucking at the hard tip. I've always been a fucking goner for a woman with curves. And Kat? She has them for days and in all the right places. Full and perfect. Tits that I did, and will again, get lost in. Hips that I want to leave marks on with how hard I squeeze them. An ass that I want to see, and maybe make a little pink, as I take her from behind.

She's perfection. And for this weekend, and hopefully longer, she's all mine.

We start to find a more even rhythm—not as rushed and frantic—when I hear the telltale sign of her stomach rumbling. I stop what I'm doing, and she goes still, as it makes the gurgling sound again.

"Have you eaten today?"

"Yes," she says slowly, though her eyes are wandering like she has to think about it. "I had a bagel this morning."

I lay down one more kiss on her chest before I prop myself up on my elbows. "How about this? We press pause to this—emphasis on pause—freshen up, go downstairs, and have our first official dinner date."

She gives me a smile that hits me right in the heart. "I like the sound of that. Even though I still contend hot dogs were a valid first dinner."

"I prefer to call it our appetizer."

That makes her smile. "I must say, I'm surprised you want to go get dinner."

"Really? Why?"

She presses into me, her chest coming in contact with mine. "I figured you'd suggest room service."

I lean back down, my lips just inches away from hers. "While that does sound amazing, if we stay in this room, I'm going to ignore your stomach and fuck you until neither of us can walk. My only meal is going to be your pussy, and you're going to have my cock for dessert. And for what I have planned, I'm going to need you well fed."

Kat is hungry in every sense of the word if her dilated eyes are any sort of signal. "You have plans?"

"Oh Kat," I say, going in for one more kiss. "So many plans."

———

As hard as it was to keep my hands off Kat while we got ready—and holy shit was it hard, given the woman literally got dressed in front of me so I know for a fact which pair of panties she chose to wear tonight—I did it. An hour later, we're walking hand-in-hand down to The Lookout, the restaurant at the Timberline Inn.

"Two?" the hostess asks.

"Yes. Table for Ross."

She checks her reservations before grabbing two menus. "Yes, Mr. Ross. Right this way."

I move my hand to the small of Kat's back as we walk through the restaurant. I keep one eye on where we're going, and another to take in as much as I can. Good ambiance. Soft lighting that's the perfect amount of not too dark and not too bright. Instrumental Christmas music filling the air, but again, at the perfect volume, so guests don't have to shout. Tea lights are on each of the tables, adding to the intimate feel of the restaurant.

"This place is gorgeous," Kat says, and now that I look at her, her gaze looks a lot like mine, taking in every little detail. She's likely doing it out of pleasure, while I'm taking mental notes of every single thing that sticks out to me, good and bad.

"It really is. The perfect place for a real first date."

"Second date."

We share a smile as the hostess puts down our menus and I take the moment to pull Kat's chair out for her.

"Why, thank you," she says as she slides in. "Quite the gentleman."

I laugh as I take a seat across from her. "In some areas."

I send her a wink, and a slight blush creeps over her cheeks as the waitress comes over to greet us. She tells us the specials for the night—including a steak dish that I'll absolutely be ordering—and we each order an old fashioned before she walks away.

Kat is still looking over the menu, but I can't stop staring at her.

"What?" she asks when she catches me.

"I just can't get over this," I say. "The chances for this to be happening have to be less than winning the lottery or hitting a royal flush on the deal."

"Probably true," she says as she closes the menu. "Did you say you're here for work?"

I nod. "Yes. Well, I'm meeting a potential new client. We're sneaking in a meeting before the holidays to see if we're going to be a fit."

"Wow. What are the odds indeed?"

"Why do you say that?"

"Because that's exactly what I'm doing."

I can tell that her brain is doing the same as mine, trying to make sense of all of these coincidences as our waitress comes back over with our drinks. Something isn't right. I have a weird feeling about this whole thing, but I can't quite put a finger on it.

"What is it you do?" I ask. "I don't think we ever talked about it."

She takes a sip of her drink before answering. "I'm in public relations. Well, more media strategy for corporate businesses. You?"

I choke on the bourbon. Because in that second, everything is coming into focus.

Why she was at speed dating.

Why she's here.

That *Kat* is short for *Katherine* and not spelled like a fucking cat.

And what I think is true is confirmed when a husky voice breaks the sudden tension.

"Look at that! Grayson Ross and Katherine Smith, the Timberline's two guests of honor, dining together. What a small world!"

What a small world indeed...

guide to christmas (and love) rule #27

Make your list. Check it twice. Because Santa knows how naughty you've been. (Even when you don't).

8

kat

I'M VERY, VERY CONFUSED.

In front of me, I have my date, who in the matter of a split-second went from charming and warm to stiff and silent. To my right there's a man who could win the New York City Santa Claus contest and apparently knows my name. Behind him is a waitress who just wants to take our orders.

I wish she could. My stomach is growling, and I have a feeling I'm about to lose my appetite.

"Grayson, Katherine, I'm glad you both could make it." Santa extends his hand as Grayson stands to shake it.

"Absolutely," Grayson says. "But I thought you were out of town all weekend. We're still meeting Monday, correct?"

Meeting Monday? I have a meeting on Monday. There seem to be a lot of meetings on Monday…

"That *was* the plan," Santa says. "But have you seen the weather report?"

Grayson shakes his head. I definitely have no clue what Santa is talking about.

"Oh, we're about to get a whopper of a snow storm," Santa says. "And right at Christmas. How poetic! It looks like Rudolph will be coming out of retirement this year!"

And he makes Christmas jokes? I'm so fucking confused, which is what I'm guessing Santa sees when he turns to talk to me.

"Katherine, so good to meet you," Santa says. "I've heard nothing but amazing things about you and your work from my son."

I stand up and smooth down my dress—a fitted one Katherine would never be seen in. Rarely do Kat and Katherine have to actually coexist, but here we go. "Hello. I'm sorry for my about-to-be rudeness, but I seem to be missing a few pages..."

Santa laughs. And I'm talking full on, stomach-like-a-bowl-full-of-cherries, laugh. "I'm sorry. I'm the rude one. Howard Williams, owner of the Timberline Inn."

"Oh," I know I sound surprised, and it's because I am. "I was told by Logan that Declan Williams was the owner."

"That would be my son, the soon-to-be owner," Howard says. "I've run this place for forty-five years. Took it over from my father, who built it with his bare hands in 1960. Though, I've always doubted that story."

I laugh. "I'm sure his blood, sweat, and tears were poured into this no matter how it happened. And I must tell you, the entire property is beautiful."

"There seems to be a lot of beauty here tonight."

Anything else I was about to say leaves my brain as a younger, and quite good-looking, man walks up next to Howard. He might not be Santa, but I can see the resemblance by their sparkling blue eyes. And if this is what Howard looked like when he was younger, then hot damn…Santa used to *get it*.

"You're too kind," I say as I extend my hand. "Katherine Smith."

"Declan Williams. A pleasure to meet you."

We exchange a handshake—it's firm, which is always a good sign. I hate when men don't grasp my hand simply because I'm a woman. I'm also ignoring the "beauty" comment he made. I don't want to make any assumptions about him either way, and even though he might be very handsome, he's not my kind of handsome.

Except the man who *is* my kind of handsome is staring at us like he wants to rip someone to shreds.

"Would you two care to join us?" I ask.

"Oh, we don't want to interrupt," Howard says.

"No, please." Grayson speaks up. "I'd love to hear how we're *all* brought together like this."

His choice of words throws me, and as we settle in, I really try to figure out what has changed in the past five minutes, other than our guests. His shoulders are tense. His expression is flat. A little angry? Or am I making that up? The vibe has definitely shifted so I don't know if he's actually mad or if I'm imagining it.

What would he be mad at? Or who? Howard interrupting? Declan's existence? Me? No. That can't be it. I mean, I've made plenty of people mad over the years. But in this case, I don't think I did anything wrong. When I piss people off, I generally like to know what I did. You know, in case I want to do it again.

"I was going to ask you the same thing," Howard says, taking a seat between Grayson and I. "I didn't realize the two people Declan and I are talking to about possible media plans knew each other."

I snap my head to Grayson then back to Howard. "Two people?"

I don't mean to say it out loud, but it slips. That's his Monday meeting? His Monday meeting is the same as my Monday meeting?

Oh now it all makes sense. That's why his demeanor changed the instant I told him what I did for a living. Why he's glaring at me with narrowed eyes. Though I feel like that reaction is a little overdramatic. I'm just his competition; nothing to get your boxers in a twist about.

Except that I've never had competition who's bent me over and fucked me in a shower.

As my brain plays catch up, every swirling thought crashes together as I fully put together the entirety of this situation:

Grayson is my competition.

He works in my industry.

Which means our relationship, or whatever this was going to be, is over before it even begins.

I swallow the lump in my throat and push back a pesky tear at the realization.

Years ago, I made a vow to myself that never again would I date inside the PR world. Not coworkers. Not competition. Not anyone. It only leads to heartbreak, deceit, and a fear of trust that will take you years to recover from.

I glance over to Grayson, who's listening intently to whatever Howard is saying. I knew things were too good to be true. I knew there was something that was going to come out of left field and wallop me upside the head.

I just never thought it would be this.

But I can't be sad about that. Not now. I have to get into Katherine mode. Especially since my adversary is looking at me like someone he's trying to take down instead of someone he's trying to go down on.

"May I ask, why did you bring two of us in?" Grayson asks. "I was under the impression from my boss at Sterling Strategies that you had just reached out to *us.*"

Sterling Strategies? They're a big deal in the Nashville PR scene. I know that most of the pitches I've gone on, they've also been trying to obtain the client. They do good work, from the campaigns I've seen. Maybe a little too standard and boring for my taste, but to each their own. They have a good rep and get the job done.

"I'm sorry if we gave that impression to you both," Howard begins. "And nothing against you, Miss Smith, but I've done business with Sterling Strategies for years. Well, as much as a family-owned inn in the Smoky Mountains can need media help. Mostly just new ways to draw in tourists, you know, that sort of thing. But every time we've called on Sterling, they've always given us great results."

"On behalf of the company, we appreciate that," Grayson says, suddenly more chummy with Howard than he was five minutes ago. "Melinda has said wonderful things about you. I'm honored she entrusted me to help you with whatever your needs are."

I didn't get the ass kisser vibes from Grayson, but here we are. Just like every other corporate bro when they see a commission...

"Thank you," Howard says. "I knew the hotel needed an upgrade, but what we did with the renovation was all Declan's idea. His vision for the property is more than I, or his grandfather, could've ever imagined."

"It's just moving ahead with the times," Declan says as he turns to me. "My goal has been to make sure that the Timberline keeps the charm and nostalgia that people have loved about it for three generations. The bricks, the wood floors and framing, the high ceilings...the rustic experience. That's our bread and butter, and I didn't want to lose that."

"I promise you didn't," I say. "This whole place is absolutely stunning."

"Thank you," he says with a flirtatious smile. Note to self: Keep Declan an arms-length away. At least until I can truly get a read on him. "But while we want to keep the same charm, it's going to be imperative that we attract new clientele. The younger generation that would rather stay in Air BnBs or a cabin in the mountains. I want to offer them high-end dining, but with an affordable price tag. Excursions. Experiences. And with those new ideas, I wanted to also bring in a new perspective. Someone who hadn't done business with us in the past and maybe could offer a fresh approach."

If I listen closely enough, I swear I can hear Grayson mumbling something under his breath.

Oh, this man is pressed…which can only give me an advantage in the long run.

"That's why I reached out to Logan," Declan continues. "He raved about you when we met at the Under-40 Business Conference last year. How you single-handedly took GameTech from the kitchen table to a billion-dollar enterprise is…it's absolutely fascinating. And, well, I don't know if we're ever going to have the word billions in our title, but I'd sure like to see what you can help us with."

"Never say never. When Logan came up with SpaceCraft, we were two dumb kids eating bad Chinese food on a wobbly kitchen table. If you have the dream, I say the sky's the limit." I turn to give a soft smile to Howard. "You and your family really have built something amazing here. I'm just going to help you come up with the best way to make sure everybody knows about it."

Grayson loudly clears his throat at my deliberate choice of words. He's so sensitive. Good to know.

"By the end of the day on Monday, you'll have the absolute best options for whatever your needs are," Grayson says. "Whether that's the brand-new idea from a person you just met, or your tried and true—and proven—option—either way, you'll be in the best hands possible."

For the first time since Howard and Declan have sat down, Grayson and I really look at each other, and not as people who are going to rip each other's clothes off later. Foes. Rivals. One winner. One loser.

Sure, there's heat between us still. But now it's about winning. I might not be overly competitive in day-to-day life, but when I know there's a prize at stake, there's no option of me not getting it. So sorry, Grayson…you might've made me squirt. You might look sexy as hell with that perfect scruff. And I might've had thoughts about taking that dark green button down you're wearing and slipping it on while you fuck me in it. But when it comes to winning and losing, I don't lose.

Ever.

"So are we still planning to meet on Monday?" I ask. "You said something earlier about the weather?"

"Yes, the original reason that we rudely interrupted your dinner," Declan says. "The snow is supposed to do its worst overnight Sunday to Monday. We were seeing, since you were both here, if we could move the meetings up to tomorrow so we can get you both out of here and not ruin your holiday."

"Of course."

Grayson and I say the same thing in unison, but he's not quick enough, so I get the next word. "Tomorrow is great."

Sure, I had plans tomorrow of being naked for most of the day and working on my presentation in between rounds, but that's now out the door.

"Excellent," Howard says, clapping his hands as he stands up. "Thank you both again for coming. Enjoy your dinner tonight. It's on us."

I tell both Howard and Declan goodnight, and Grayson does the same. We both sit back down and there's silence between us. Neither of us are blinking. No one wants to break first.

No one wants to lose.

Oh Grayson...this weekend just got a different kind of fun.

9

grayson

"What the fuck, Kat? Or is it Katherine? Apparently I don't even know your name!"

Because the hotel door slow closes on itself, I don't have the privilege to take my frustrations out by slamming it, but I wish I could. I feel like I've been losing it for the past hour. Between finding out that Kat is, in fact, Katherine Smith, the woman who I've declared my nemesis; Howard and Declan inviting themselves to our meal; Declan looking at Kat like *she's* his next meal…I was about to fucking blow. I don't like feeling this out of control. Sure, I'm all for spontaneousness and a good, unpredictable adventure, but that's because it's *my choice*. I'm the one who says it's okay to see where the wind takes me. But this right here? This is just fucking insanity.

"Newsflash: Kat is short for Katherine. So you do know my name. And now you know both of them." She steps closer to me, clearly ready for the battle that she and I both know we're about to have. "Also, I feel like the generic question of 'what the fuck' could mean many different things. How about we get a little more specific? You know, because I wouldn't want you to become any *more* confused than you clearly are."

I'm still breathing heavy, trying to calm myself to the night's events. But then there's Kat, or Katherine, whatever she wants to be called, who looks cool, calm and collected. She's taking off her earrings one by one and slipping out of her heels. The sarcasm is oozing in her voice.

She's my rival. My adversary. The woman who's beaten me on many occasions.

And yet, I still want to fuck her. Which is a really, really, big problem.

"How about we start with you not telling me who you were?" I ask, plenty of snark and anger in my tone. "Or should I just call you Vixen, since that's what you are?"

She laughs at that. "When did I lie to you about my identity? Please, lay out your defense. Also, why the fuck am I a reindeer?"

"Not that kind of vixen," I say, getting more frustrated because of how much she's throwing me off my game. "Like a fox. Sneaky. You know. A vixen! Because you weren't up front about everything."

Her eyebrows raise slightly as she takes a few steps in my direction. Her eyes are set on me, and it looks like she's locking in for battle. Good, because this is what it's about to be. "When we met, I told you my name, which is the shortened version of my full name that I go by in social settings. My apologies for not knowing that at a speed-dating event where we had seven minutes to get to know each other, that I didn't give you my full government name, Social Security number, and my mother's maiden name. I'll remember that for next time. Should I include my first pet to be safe?"

"But you weren't there for speed dating," I say in a huff. "You were there to impress Hazel."

"Pot calling the kettle black, wouldn't you say?" She steps even closer, our bodies nearly touching with every breath we take. "How did that go, by the way? Get the client?"

Red. That's all I'm seeing right now. Yet, I don't know which part of this I'm angrier about, the fact that I'm meeting my rival, that she's nothing like I'd envisioned, that she's right about a lot of things, or that I want to fuck her.

Honestly, it's all of the above.

"Why didn't you tell me you worked in PR?"

"I could ask you the same question," she says. "Because again, I also seemed to have learned downstairs that you work for a public relations firm, which was brand-new information. So before we go out throwing stones, Grayson, how about we realize that we're maybe a both a little in the dark about who we are and maybe, just maybe, we've taken things a little fast and we need to play catch up."

Why does she have to be sensible?

I pace around the room for a few seconds, taking some deep breaths and trying to calm myself down. Because right now I'm feeling a thousand emotions, and I don't know which ones are warranted.

"How about I start while you get your steps in," she says. How does she make a joke that's a dig at me, while also making me laugh? I thought the moment I met her that she was going to be the death of me; I just didn't realize how multi-faceted that statement was.

"My name is Katherine Smith. I go by Kat, except in professional settings. I'm about to turn thirty years old, I'm an Aries, and have been in public relations and media strategies since I graduated college. I'm currently an independent strategist while also serving as head of PR for GameTech Industries. I think deep dish pizza is really just a casserole, and on that note, the elite pizza toppings are pepperoni and mushrooms. I also believe that you should have to work a shift at a grocery store if you don't return your shopping cart, that everything can be fixed with an iced coffee, and 'Jingle Bells' is the worst Christmas carol in existence."

"Bold take," I say. "Clearly that right answer is 'Twelve Days of Christmas.' What day does it actually start? When does it end? Why are there so many birds involved?"

This stops her train of thought. "You're right. So many fucking birds. Who would even want them?"

"Right?"

She smiles at me. Smiles! I mean, I'm smiling too, but how dare she! I'm trying to be mad at her. Now I just want to kiss her.

"Have we calmed down yet?" she asks, patting the bed for me to take a seat next to her. "And maybe gotten under control the douche that popped out at the table in front of Howard and Declan?"

I nod and finally let myself stop moving for a second, sitting down on the bed—*the only bed in our room*—as I take a second and let every ounce of information finally settle in.

She's my competition.

She's my rival—the only person since I transferred to Nashville to get the best of me.

She's the woman I'm fucking crazy about.

One of those things is not like the other.

"I'm sorry about that," I say, finally feeling like my blood pressure is back to a normal level. "I felt overwhelmed and bombarded."

"I get that," she says. "How about you tell me about yourself, now that we're doing reintroductions?"

I take in a breath before beginning. "I'm Grayson Ross. I don't go by any other names, so there's no confusing me. I'm thirty-four and work for Sterling Strategies as a public relations and media specialist. I think I'm a Leo, but only because a girl I met on a blind date said I was. I'm originally from Connecticut and moved to Nashville three years ago. I'm a baseball fanatic—played in college, have a collection of baseball cards, and my bucket list is to visit every stadium in the country. I could eat tacos for every meal, I never skip out on the queso, pineapple gets too much hate for being on pizza, and you, Katherine Smith, are the only person since I've transferred to Nashville who has ever beaten me out for a client."

My admission takes her off guard. "Are you serious?"

"As a heart attack," I say. "I've had a pretty good run here. Undefeated in every sense of the word. Worked with some celebrities, cleaned up a situation that could've sent the country music world into a spiral, handled a few brand deals and new business rollouts. I was on the roll of a lifetime. Then one day, I got the email that no person in our business wants to get."

"The decline?"

I tap my nose. "The very one. But I didn't let it bother me. No one can bat a thousand, you know?"

"I don't. I'm assuming that's a baseball reference? All I know about the sport is that a baseball stadium is an acceptable place to eat unlimited hot dogs."

God, I want to kiss her. I want to be having this get-to-know-you conversation with her wrapped in my arms—preferably naked. But unfortunately, that now can't happen. Not now. Not ever.

If there's one thing I know about this industry it's that you can't sleep with the enemy. And that's exactly what this beautiful vixen is.

"In baseball, batting a thousand is a perfect average. But in comparison, an average of three-hundred gets you into the Hall of Fame. A four-hundred is considered off the charts."

"That feels like a pretty low success rate."

I laugh. "I can see that. But my success rate in the corporate world? I was having a Hall-of-Fame career. So, one loss didn't bother me. I knew the streak was gonna have to end at some point."

"I'm sorry?"

I appreciate the question mark she added, even though I know she's not. At least, I wouldn't be. "It wasn't that one that rattled me; it was when I went to talk to the higher-ups at Pittman Dean. The client I knew I wasn't going to get beaten out on."

"Really? How did you know you were going to win over the

biggest bank in Nashville? A cocky attitude like that never bodes well."

Her sarcasm used to be endearing. Now it's maddening. But that's because I can't kiss the smirk off her face.

"I knew, or I thought I knew, because two of my friends were on the hiring committee. Did I go into it maybe a little cocky? Sure, but I knew exactly what they wanted. I knew what they needed to do to turn their image around after what their CEO did."

Her smile only widens. "Just to make sure I'm not confused again—you know, because of all the confusion tonight—what did happen with that?"

I narrow my eyes. "Some woman named Katherine Smith got the job and somehow made the CEO disappear into the night while also turning the bank's profits around in an instant."

"Damn. She does good work."

"So I've been told."

We sit for a second, our eyes locked, and I know she wants to kiss me. Hell, I want to kiss her. But I can't. I need to get used to that.

"In my defense," she says, "that wasn't my first cheating CEO fire I've had to put out. I had experience, brought in those ideas, found some new things that were going to work in this climate, and poof, you have a company with profits back up and a CEO whose name we've already forgotten."

"Rationally I know this. But it wasn't even two weeks after that miss that you did it again."

"Are you kidding me? I also beat you out on the tech bros?"

"You did."

"Holy shit," she says, not believing it either. "So, to wrap this up: I've beaten you four times in a row, a streak that had seen zero losses until I got bored working for Logan and decided to venture out for myself. You did some digging, because you were big mad that someone was beating you, found my name, and I became your Lex Luthor."

"I wouldn't go that far," I say. Her eyebrow raise clearly says that she doesn't believe me. "Okay, maybe a little. I wanted to find out who you were. What made you better than me. I was determined not to lose to you again. And during that, I declared you my nemesis."

Her eyes are big like an idea just hit her. "Did you go to the speed dating event to find me?"

I quickly shake my head. "No. I promise I didn't. I went there because I thought it would impress Hazel that I took the extra initiative. Turns out I wasn't the only one with that idea."

Her shoulders relax. "Great minds think alike."

I hate that a few hours ago, that phrase had a completely different meaning. "So they do."

We sit in silence for at least a minute, letting the dust settle. While part of me feels better that a lot has been cleared up, there's now a new set of questions.

Ones I'm pretty sure I'm not going to like the answers to.

"Suddenly these sleeping arrangements don't feel like they're the best idea," she says.

I shake my head. "I'll call down to the front desk to see if they can bring me a cot."

She nods, but doesn't say anything else. I think we're both thinking the same thing; the question is who's going to say it first. Judging by the sad look in her eyes, one I know I'm mirroring, we both know where this is, and isn't, leading.

"I think it's best if after we get back to Nashville, that..."

"We stop things before they ever get started."

I nod, grateful she was able to finish it. "I think it's best for both of us."

"Agree." She pauses for a second to take in a deep breath. "I don't date inside the business. Not coworkers. Not competition. It's...the lines are too blurred, and it gets too messy."

"That's understandable," I say. "I told my boss that you were my nemesis. It'd be weird if I brought you to the holiday party."

This makes her laugh. "It's just smart if we cut our losses before things get serious."

She's right again. And again, I hate it. "You're right. You are my competition."

"I'm the enemy."

"That sounds really harsh," I say. "Rival feels less like I want you dead."

"Exactly. And I don't want you dead either…"

"I just want your clients."

"Every single one of them."

The stare down each of us gives the other is both competitive and fueled with tension. Honestly, getting over how to look at her and not kiss her might be harder than figuring out how to beat her.

"Tomorrow is going to be nuts with finalizing projects while also meeting with Howard and Declan," she says. "I think it'll be best if we keep separated."

"Agree," I say. "The restaurant is plenty big enough that we can find a table and separate ourselves."

"And if it's too busy, I'll go to the lobby," she says. "Bedroom is an off-limits work zone. That way we can come and go as we please without having to worry about someone stumbling onto something they shouldn't."

"Exactly. Don't want to copy off of anyone's paper."

I see her flinch to those words, which I didn't think was anything bad, so I quickly change the direction of the conversation.

"We'll keep our distance as much as we can. We'll only have to deal with our sleeping situation for one night, and then we'll be on our way to our respective holiday destinations."

"And when we get back to Nashville, we'll just go back to how things were before this week. Just two PR strategists bidding for the same clients."

"Two rivals."

"Nothing more. Nothing less."

Her words hit me like a knife to the chest. It's logical. It makes sense. I'm too competitive to date someone in the industry, and even if I weren't, it's a hard limit for her. We wouldn't work. Better to know that now rather than later.

Right?

"It's getting late," I say. "I should call down to the front desk to see about the cot and some extra pillows and blankets."

Kat nods and stands up off the bed. "I'll use the bathroom first, if that's okay?"

It takes a second for either of us to move, and it takes longer for me to make it to the phone after Kat gathers her toiletries and pajamas.

"Hi, this is Grayson Ross in room 403. I was wondering if there's a cot available that can be used?"

"Oh yes!" the attendant says in the most cheerful voice I've ever heard. Probably because she's still panicking that I'm going to call and scream at her for the mix-up. "We'll have it up to you right away."

My stomach sinks with her words. Part of me hoped that, like the rooms in this hotel, a cot suddenly wouldn't be available. That…oh no…I guess I'd have to sleep in the same bed as Kat. Yes, that would've made me the definition of a glutton for punishment after our conversation. But I selfishly want one more night. Even if I can't hold her, or kiss her, or make her scream where the sound lives rent-free in my head, I wanted one more night of just being near her.

But no…now the hotel has amenities. Thanks, Timberline…

"All yours," I hear Kat say as she comes out of the bathroom.

"Thanks." I purposefully don't look at her as I gather my things. I'm not ready to see her choice of nightwear. "The cot is coming up if someone knocks at the door."

I quickly turn around, still not paying attention to anything around me, which is how I don't realize until it's too late that I'm walking into Kat.

Neither of us move, both too stunned, and maybe, too stupid, to move. God, I want to kiss her. Now I'm glad I have the cot because it's the only thing that I know is going to make me be on my best behavior tonight.

"Sorry," she says as she steps away, which is when I see she's wearing a Biggie Smalls T-shirt that's cut at the neck, showcasing a shoulder that my lips are dying to kiss. The sleep shorts she's wearing barely cover her ass, which of course makes my cock hate the responsible me that has declared this woman off limits. Her face is clean of makeup, and her hair is on the top of her head.

This sucks so fucking bad…

"Kat…"

I don't mean for my voice to hit that low tone, but I can't help it.

"Yes?"

"If you don't move in the next three seconds, I'm going to kiss you. And if I kiss you, I can't promise I'm going to stop at that."

I watch the blush hit her cheeks as she swallows a lump in her throat. And then, with sad eyes, she does what I ask and steps aside.

I hate that she listened.

I hate that we're being responsible.

I hate every fucking thing about this.

guide to christmas (and love) rule #87

You should get extra Christmas presents for resisting the man you can't have. Especially when he's wrapped in just a towel.

10
kat

I DIDN'T SLEEP A WINK LAST NIGHT.

For one, having a huge bed is a little off-putting when you're by yourself. Don't get me wrong—the bed was one of the most comfortable I've ever slept in. The sheets and comforter kept me warm. The mattress was firm but soft enough that I melted into it. But who I really wanted to keep me warm was sleeping on a cot that was too small for him, all while making noises that let me know just how uncomfortable he was.

He didn't ask to come to the bed. I didn't offer. We both knew where it would lead if we pried open that door.

No, the cot is the best decision for our situation.

I fucking hate that cot.

I did feel bad. Every time sleep started to find me, another sound of pain echoed in the room. Could've been his back. Might've also been my heart. It's anyone's guess at the moment.

How has this happened? For the first time in my life, I met someone whom I connected with on every level. Banter? Top tier. Chemistry? Off the charts. I know it was stupid, but tonight, before we went to dinner, and Grayson's mouth was devouring me, I thought to myself that this was my Christmas present. That

Santa knew I didn't ask for a relationship, but he still gave it to me anyway.

Joke's on me. I feel like the old Charlie Brown scenario where all the kids are saying what they got for Christmas, and all I got was a rock.

I haven't moved from the bed. Grayson's in the shower; at least, that's what I'm guessing based on the sounds coming from the bathroom, when I hear my phone vibrating on the nightside table.

LOGAN

Everything okay? Haven't heard from you but also just heard about the weather coming through.

KAT

I'm fine. Ready to be out of here.

Why? What happened?

I debate how much to tell him. My best friend has always been protective of me, especially when it comes to dating. I didn't have any brothers to give high school boys side-eyes for liking me, and I didn't live with my dad during my teenage dating years. Needless to say, my best friend has embraced those roles as personal missions.

So as much as I want to tell him everything that happened yesterday, unless I want a British billionaire to show up in the next hour via his private jet, I'll just give him the abbreviated version.

Remember how I told you not to get your hopes up about Grayson?

Oh no...what happened?

He works in PR.

And that's all I need to say. Logan knows everything that happened back then. He knows what kind of relationship I was in, and why I needed out so bad. How I almost lost my career because of it. Sometimes I think he hired me at GameTech just to get me out of that situation.

I'm so sorry, Kat. You really seemed to like him.

I did, but better to find out early. No attachments.

Wait...was I a jinx?

I laugh, because honestly, I had the same thought sometime around 4:18 in the morning, give or take three minutes. Because I swear this happens every time: The second I tell Logan about a guy...BOOM. He's gone in a week. Usually it's ghosting or finding out that they're married. This was new territory.

You're not a jinx. This was going to happen no matter when I told you.

Wait. How did you find out?

Remember when I asked you if there was anyone else Declan was talking to?

I do and...NO!

Yes. He's here as well.

I specifically leave out the sleeping arrangements part. We don't need to get into all of that.

I'm sorry, Kat. Let me know if there's anything I can do. Or if you need someone to vent to. I'm here.

> Actually, the reservations that you got me to St. Lucia. Can they be moved up? I'd love to get out of here before the snow hits.

Not a problem. The jet will be waiting for you. I'll call the hotel and adjust your stay.

> Thanks. You're the best.

Anytime. Let me know if you need anything else.

I set down my phone just as I hear the sound of the water turning off. Okay, no more thinking about what could've been with Grayson and me. Men come and go, but a new client means a new designer handbag. And I'll never say no to a new Louis.

I roll myself out of bed and give myself an internal pep talk. I'm not going to wallow anymore about what could've been. No, it's time for Katherine to enter the chat and serve up the best damn pitch a family-owned hotel has ever listened to.

Because I don't like losing. Especially when I know there's a target on my back.

A target I want to kiss a little.

I don't want to be just standing around when he comes out of the bathroom, so I go over to my suitcase and start digging for clothes. It's a Katherine day, which means beige bra, plain underwear, a pair of leggings, and an oversized sweater that hangs just off my shoulder for the day. I'll change into my professional clothes before it's time to present.

I turn around with the clothes in my hand, and somehow, I didn't hear the bathroom door click open. Which is why I jump out of my skin when I see Grayson walking out.

Sonofabiscuit...

Is he doing this on purpose? He has to be. Because he's wearing a towel that's wrapped around his waist and holding on for dear fucking life. There's water still dripping from his chest, and his hair is damp. And the best/worst part...there's steam literally following him out of the bathroom. I thought that could only happen on that one television show.

"Fucking hell…" I whisper, dropping the clothes I'm holding. Because apparently I've lost all brain function.

"You okay?" he asks, a cocky smirk on his handsome face. Wait. Why is he back to cocky Grayson? "Need some help there?"

Oh, this motherfucker did this on purpose…

I know this, yet I can't stop staring and thinking what he could *actually* help with. The towel falling would help me a lot. It means I wouldn't have to dig into my memory to remember what his cock looked like. And a morning blow job helps everyone, really.

No! Stop that! Be-fucking-have!

Which is why the only word that comes out of my mouth is "Nope!" as I bend down, pick up my clothes, and sprint to the bathroom.

"You sure?"

"Yup!" I slam the door behind me. I can hear Grayson chuckling outside as I try to catch my breath.

Because everything's not okay. Everything fucking sucks.

11
grayson

Now that is what I call a productive morning.

I left the hotel room before Kat could come back out—I knew I had the upper hand after my not-so-accidental shower move—and headed down to the coffee shop at the hotel. I found the perfect booth, got a sandwich and the best Americano I've had in a while, and put together a presentation that's going to wow Declan and Howard.

From the second I sat down, the ideas started pouring from me. Podcasts. YouTube channels. Travel channel shows. That's what's going to put the Timberline on the national map. Unfortunately, I know who I work for, and they're going to want to make sure I include the tried-and-true methods.

Or as I call them, boring. Local media buys. Making the rounds with the local television and radio stations. That kind of approach. I hate having to keep going back to that, but when your boss tells you to include them, you do.

Hopefully, it doesn't put me behind whatever ideas Kat's coming up with.

No, I'm not going to worry about her. I can only control what I'm doing, and what I can do is give them the best options—or as I'm calling it, a little bit of everything—and head into the holiday with a win. And if it's a win that makes my family partially proud of me and beats Kat—wait, Katherine—than all the better.

With a huge feeling of confidence, I close my laptop, knowing that it's time to get a move on for my meeting. It's just before noon, and as long as the restaurant isn't too busy, I'll be able to grab a sandwich before heading back to the room to get ready.

"Sit wherever you'd like," one of the waitresses says. "It's open seating at lunch."

"Thank you." I look around the restaurant, eyeing my choice of tables. I spy one along the window, giving me a fantastic view of the mountains, but then I realize who's also grabbing a bite.

Kat. Who's having lunch with Declan.

What. The. Fuck.

I glare at the two of them, who I don't think have realized I'm here, as I pull out my chair and take a seat. Though, I should invite myself to sit with them. Declan had no problem doing it last night, might as well repay the favor.

I don't. No, I opt to sit six tables away and just glare. Not something I should be doing to the man I need to like me and my presentation in an hour. Or something I should be doing to a woman who has said loud and clear that we don't have a future together. Yet, I can't seem to help it.

The feelings I have for Kat, Katherine, whatever the hell her name is, are conflicting as hell. Because how do I in one breath want to beat her professionally, but in the next, pull her into my arms and never let her go? I know she said that in professional settings she goes by Katherine, and part of me wishes that's how we could be. That Katherine and Grayson could be rivals by day, but Kat and Grayson could be together by night.

It sounds like a storyline out of a fantasy book. Then again, that's all Kat and I can ever be—a fantasy.

"What can I get for you?" the waitress who greeted me earlier asks.

"Club sandwich and an iced tea," I grit out, my eyes still trained on the two of them.

Luckily, the waitress picks up that I'm not especially chatty and walks away. For real, though, what the hell are they talking about? Why is she laughing? He can't be that funny. Did they move up their meeting? No, that wouldn't make sense, as Howard's nowhere to be seen. Are they friends? Did they have a relationship before this past weekend? No, I remember them saying that he knew Logan, but the two of them had never met.

I watch them closely, trying to get a read on their body language. Is he hitting on her? I mean, I get why if he is. She's a beautiful woman. I thought he was flirting last night—it's why I've been acting the way I have—but looking at them now, I don't get that vibe. Neither of them are leaning into each other. Sure, she's laughing at something he said. He's smiling as well as he cuts up a piece of his chicken. Nothing seems out of line.

Then again, if he is, it's wildly inappropriate. She's presenting to him later. He's a decision-maker for this business. It's an imbalance in the power dynamic, and it's shitty if he's trying to exploit her as a woman to use to his business advantage. I've seen men in my own company do this, and it's fucking horse shit. If I knew that someone ever did that to my sister, I'd tear them limb from limb. Then again, my sister would stomp on their dicks, tie them up in lawsuits, and smile about it as she walked away in ridiculously high heels.

Now that I calm myself a bit, I don't see Kat allowing that to happen either. She's a smart woman. Quick to pick up on things. And clearly can hold herself in the business world.

Wait…why do I care? I shouldn't. Sure, I want to make sure their meeting isn't giving her an unfair advantage in the business sense, but personally, I shouldn't give two shits.

Except I do. Because as much as I know things could never work between us, I can't turn off the switch when it comes to this woman.

I shake my head a bit, trying concentrate on anything except the two of them. I get lost in the notes I left for myself on my phone when I hear Kat's laughter coming toward me.

"Oh! Grayson!" she says cheerily. "When did you get here?"

"Few minutes ago," I say through gritted teeth. Because apparently I have no other way of talking when the two of them are together. "You two had lunch?"

Declan holds up his hands in surrender. "She was eating alone, and I thought she could use some company. I promise we didn't talk about anything to do with the job. That wouldn't be fair."

My gut reaction is to believe him. I should be happier about that than I am. "So what did you two talk about?"

My pettiness might be able to take a back seat, but my curiosity can't.

"I was telling him about my trip to St. Lucia for Christmas," Kat says. "Turns out he's been there and he was giving me some sights to see. Well, the ones that don't have me going on an all-day excursion."

"Do you know this woman isn't an excursion girl?" he asks. "She'd rather lay on the beach all day then go hike the trails and mountains."

"I did," I say, puffing my chest out a little. "I believe she likes to call herself 'outside-y, not outdoorsy.'"

The smile she gives me hits me square in the chest. Neither of us say anything as we share a knowing look, until Declan breaks the silence.

"I need to get back to the office. See you both shortly."

I nod. "See you then."

We both watch Declan walk away, but neither of us go anywhere.

"You remembered."

I could play it coy, but I chose not to. "I remember everything."

My words seem to surprise her as our gazes lock. The heat and want and desire that passes through us in this moment is overwhelming. I know she can feel it. I see her eyes swirling with emotion. I imagine it's how mine look.

We both want each other. But we both know the line in the sand is drawn. We can't.

And it fucking sucks.

I want to kiss her. I want it more than my next breath. I want to say fuck our jobs, fuck everything that I thought, fuck whatever is holding her back, and just kiss her. Take her in my arms and never let her go. Run off to that beach in St. Lucia and start a life selling rental chairs on a beach.

And I'm about to. I'm this close to taking a step in when the sound of Santa Claus breaks our spell.

"Ho! Ho! Ho!"

Kat and I both turn to see Howard coming through the lobby, Santa suit on, despite it still being three days before Christmas. I'm distracted for just a few seconds, but it's long enough to give Kat an opening to leave. When I notice, she's already half way to the elevator, power-walking away like her life depends on it.

I want to run after her. I want to recreate the elevator magic that I know we have.

But I can't.

I have a job to do.

And for the first time in my professional life, I want to say "fuck the job."

———

Nailed it.

I don't know how a presentation could've gone any better. I even genuinely smiled at Declan and had a great discussion with him about utilizing influencers. It spun off into a conversation about all the things people can do in the Smoky Mountains that I had no idea about. The Northeastern guy in me just thought it was hiking and horseback riding.

He's not so bad I guess. At least, when Kat's not involved.

I walk to the elevator to head back to the room riding a high, but as soon as the elevator door closes, I feel the crash from the adrenaline wearing off starting to hit. It's been a chaotic forty-eight hours, and all I want right now is a hot shower and a solid nap. I barely slept last night and have a feeling the same will be true tonight.

I check my watch to see that it's just before four o'clock. My guess is that Kat is probably in the room—AKA the neutral zone —getting ready for her presentation. I should leave her alone. When she ran from the lobby earlier to the elevator, I assumed she'd be here, but I didn't see her when I came up to get ready. But I have no plans on messing with her, or even engaging in conversation. She can do what she needs to get ready as long as she'll let me borrow the bed for two hours to take the best nap of my life before I have to drive to Knoxville to catch my flight to Connecticut.

When I open the door to our room, I'm immediately struck by music playing from the bathroom. I don't know why, but I expected that if Kat was listening to music while getting ready for a presentation, she'd have on some sort of rap music. Maybe a pregame warmup kind of playlist. But no, the song that's playing now is a sultry one, deep tones that hit you square in the chest.

Or maybe it's hitting me because of the vision I'm looking at.

I don't mean to stare at Kat through the crack in the bathroom door that gives a view of the mirror, but it's the first thing I see when I walk in the room. She's wearing nothing but a nude color bra and panties while putting on her makeup—though she doesn't need an ounce of it.

The makeup reminds me of the first night we met. It's subtle. Her eyeliner isn't as drastic as when I saw her here at the Timberline that first day. Her lipstick isn't bold at all, yet still has a power to it. Her hair is back into a tight bun, screaming queen of the board room.

And then it hits me. *This* is Katherine Smith. This is the

persona she wears when she's in work mode. First I thought Katherine was just her more formal name, which is why she went by it professionally, but now I'm thinking it's much deeper than that. That this woman keeps business and pleasure so separate that she has to go by another name to help her compartmentalize.

I wonder why? Is it just a preference? Did something happen? Is that why she has the rules in place? Holy shit…that first night…she introduced herself as Kat. Her hair was down. But it was this subtle makeup. Beige lingerie.

That night I was with *both* these women. One my nemesis, the other my obsession. And I don't know which one I'm more attracted to.

Transfixed by the scene before me, I drop my bookbag at the doorway, my idea for a nap long gone. It's like I can't stop myself from walking toward her. She's a magnet pulling me in. I'm almost to the door when she finally makes eye contact with me, but she doesn't tell me to stop. She doesn't tell me to stay away. She doesn't say anything. She doesn't need to. Our eyes do all the talking.

We want each other. We want each other so fucking bad neither of us can stand it. But more than that, we want to win. It's where we're both alike. Neither of us are going to give in; neither of us are going to cross that line. But dammit if we're both not going to walk that line like the tightrope it is.

I push open the door, and she makes no attempt to stop me. I step behind her, taking in her perfect body through the mirror, like it's on display just for me. I can't help but look straight at her chest, her full tits propped up perfectly in a nude lace bra. The boy shorts she's wearing match, and I have to bite the inside of my cheek not to rip them down her legs so I can see if she's wet for me. I'm not even touching her, but I can see the goosebumps forming on her skin. I can tell from the defiant look in her eye that she's trying to will them away, but it's a losing effort.

"How'd it go?" she asks in an attempt to reclaim the upper hand.

"Good," I say as I step closer, allowing our bodies to touch ever so slightly. Just enough to ignite the spark that always lies between us without setting the room on fire.

"Enough to win?"

I know she's trying to taunt me with her question—it's what I would do if the roles were reversed—but I know how well I did. Which is why I can play this cool. "I like my chances."

I step closer into her, allowing my hardening cock to barely rub against her. God, what I wouldn't give to bend her over this counter and fuck her from behind. Be able to watch her face as I drive into her. Take that bun out of her hair while my dick is buried inside of her, wrapping her black hair around my hand and pulling on it, arching her back as she screams my name.

But I don't. I don't cross the line. As much as I'm dying to.

"We can't do this," she says.

"I know."

My voice is low in her ear, barely above a whisper. We're still not touching, but the heat radiating between us is enough to start a fire that would set this hotel into a blaze.

"We should walk away."

"I know."

But neither of us do, not until the timer goes off on Kat's phone, which I'm guessing is the alarm signaling that she has to go to meet with Declan and Howard.

I step away, allowing Kat to exit the bathroom before I lock myself inside. I don't even wait until she leaves before I turn on the shower to the coldest setting I can stand. I pray that she's left when I start jacking off, needing relief because of the woman who's going to be the death of me.

She's my competition.

She's my dream woman.

And I have a feeling she's going to be my biggest heartbreak.

guide to christmas (and love) rule #34

Hot tubs are the perfect addition for a snowed-in staycation. Unless they're with the man you can't have.

12
kat

Fucking. Nailed. It.

Don't get me wrong—I'm usually confident when I leave presentations. I can get a pretty good read on a room and have a gut intuition if in a few days I'm going to get the "thanks for coming" email or the celebratory phone call.

And I'd bet my vinyl collection that I'm getting that phone call sometime between Christmas and New Year's.

I insert my key card to the door and slowly open it, not sure if Grayson is still in the room. I hope he isn't. It'll make my getaway all that much easier.

I also hope he is.

I don't know when I'm going to see him again. Maybe we'll pass each other in a business office, one coming to and one going from a meeting. Maybe we'll randomly run into each other at a coffee shop. But if we do, it won't be the same. It'll be an awkward wave followed by the knowledge that something that could've been great had to end before it started.

Because it does. It's better this way. Even if it doesn't feel like it right now.

When I walk into the room, it's dead silent. Which is good. I'm going to quickly change, pack, and get the hell out of here before the snow really hits, and tomorrow I'll be waking up in St. Lucia.

As I drop my tote on the bed and slide off my heels, I hear the vibration come from my cell phone.

LOGAN

I'm so sorry.

Um…that's ominous.

KAT

For what?

I just got a call from the pilot. They're shutting down the airports.

They're what?!

I take four quick steps to the window and throw open the curtains. Oh, hell…it's really coming down. I didn't look much outside today, but I swear it wasn't coming down like this earlier.

Apparently the storm was supposed to hit overnight, but made it to your neck of the woods about ten hours early. I'll keep you posted, but it looks like you're stuck at the Timberline for a few days.

I don't even bother to answer. Instead I let out a scream that might get security called for a welfare check.

How is this happening? Not only am I not going to the beach, but I'm going to be stuck in this room with the man who is the definition of temptation?

I drop to the bed and bury my head in my hands as I come to terms with the situation. I mean, best case scenario, is that we're delayed a day and the snow will stop and everything will open up again by Christmas Eve.

Worst case scenario, I die in this room from sexual frustration and the unfairness of life.

Something in the middle will probably be what happens, but I like to know the ends of my spectrum.

I look up, and I swear the cot is staring at me. I wonder if the hotel has any rooms open? People had to have left ahead of the storm, right? Maybe I'll go ask. But if they don't, I should be nice and sleep on it tonight. The poor man suffered last night, and even though I can't date him, and I want to get this account because I'm competitive to my core, I don't want the man to suffer. Consider it my last-ditch effort to get put on the nice list. Because if Santa can read a person's mind, then he knows that in the last week, there's been a whole lot of naughty rolling through it.

Let's also call it what it is—my way of saying that I'm sorry that whatever we have between us can't go anywhere. So the least I can do is let you sleep in the bed.

I let myself fall back into the mattress and close my eyes. Yes, I might be laying down now, but I don't even have to concentrate that hard to feel him behind me like he was today in front of the mirror. I can feel his breath on my neck. His cock against my ass. Does he have any idea how bad I wanted to say to hell with my rules? That I wanted him to bend me over the counter and fuck me until I couldn't walk? I didn't care what time it was or what I had to do at that moment. All I wanted was him.

That thought makes me sit straight up. Because that wasn't a very Katherine-like thought. No, that was all Kat. If my alarm hadn't gone off, I would've initiated a move. I felt my resolve snapping. If he would've beat me to it, I wouldn't have pushed him away. Sure, I was in Katherine mode—bun and boring bra and all—and still that wasn't enough for me to resist the feelings I have for Grayson Ross.

And that's the most terrifying thought of them all.

I told myself never again. I wouldn't put myself in a situation where I could be used personally for professional gain. I put on a strong face to Logan and to anyone who knew the situation all those years ago, but inside, I'm still recovering. It's why I can't make myself trust Grayson. I want to. I don't think he's the kind of person who would do what Jeff did, but I don't know if I can risk it.

Not with my career as Katherine. And certainly not my heart as Kat.

I saw the moment he realized the difference between the two. It wasn't anything specific, but just something in his eyes told me he saw past the weak facade. Sure, he knows Kat intimately—the brazen, opinionated, says what's on her mind, doesn't care what people think girl at the bar. That's who he met first. That's who he went to the hotel with. That's who I want to be with him.

The problem is that Katherine is very much in existence, and today, he truly saw her for the first time. Not as a rival or a competitor, but as a woman. Strangely enough, I feel like he knew her intimately as well. Because when the beige bra comes out and the hair is in the bun, Kat is far away. Katherine is sensible. Hard working. A touch OCD and a whole lot of Type A. She doesn't take prisoners in the board room and will give you an idea so good you'll think it's your own, but you have no idea how you came up with it.

Katherine doesn't stand in front of a man basically naked. She doesn't risk presentations for a little midday dick. And she definitely doesn't fall for men who could ruin her career. Yet today, she was going to.

Damnit, I was going to…

"Snap out of it," I order myself as I start pacing around the hotel room. "He's just a man!"

I need out of here. If the airports are closed, I'm guessing so are the roads. Tonight is going to be torture, sharing this room with him again, which is why I have to get out, even if for just a little bit. I walk over to my suitcase, ready to shed the pantsuit that I wore today, when I notice the bathing suit I packed for St. Lucia. I never planned on using it here, and now who knows if

I'm going to use it there, but I have walked past a hot tub a few times today. Right now, the jets and a steaming hot water sound like the perfect remedy.

Twenty minutes later, I'm walking through the lobby. I make my way over to the desk, planning to ask about a second room, when I see that the line is ten deep. I also overhear that due to the storm, guests are staying longer and workers that can't make it to the hotel. Meaning they're at capacity.

Yup. It's the cot for me tonight.

Trying to make the best of things, I allow myself to take in the decor of the lobby and main room—both are absolutely stunning. Since Logan married an interior designer, I've learned a new appreciation for what it actually takes to turn a space into a masterpiece. Whoever designed and decorated the Timberline needs to have a spread in a magazine.

Shit. I should've included that in my presentation today. I grab my phone to make a note of it so when I get the job, I can add it to our ideas board. Since my head is in my phone, I'm not really paying attention to where I'm going, but I do know that the indoor pool, and hot tub, are down the hall to my right.

I'm just about finished typing when I bump the door open with my shoulder. Luckily, it's quiet when I enter—AKA no screaming kids. Except when I listen a little closer, I hear music playing softly.

Son of a bitch…

I came here to get away from thoughts of Grayson. Yet, in the hot tub, playing a song that's in my 'Wrapped' playlist at the end of every year, is the very man I apparently can't get away from.

He doesn't see me yet. He's sitting in the steaming water, eyes closed, head back—and, of course, shirtless. I could run. I *should* run. I can head back upstairs—or maybe to the bar for a shot or ten—and pretend this never happened.

Or, I could put on my big girl pants, get in the hot tub like I planned, and start figuring out a way to resist Grayson Ross. Who knows how long we're going to be snowed in. I probably need to figure out how to coexist with him while also resisting the urge to jump him.

I start slowly making my way to the hot tub when his eyes open. It doesn't take them long to spot me, and I swear, once they do, my body temperature changes in an instant. Sure, that could be attributed to the humidity of the pool and hot tub, but it's not that. No, this is only a sensation I feel when Grayson's hazel eyes are on me.

A feeling I have to learn to resist, and also figure out how not to crave.

"Great minds?"

That seems to be the running joke between us, and while it's true, it's just another reminder of how great I think we could be together if the circumstances were different.

"Something like that," I say as casual as I can, setting down my tote bag as I step out of my sandals. I purposefully don't look at him while I slip off the shorts I wore over the bathing suit I decided to put on—a one-piece with a halter neck that gives fifties retro vibes, polka dots and all. I might not be looking at him, but I feel his eyes on me. Which is a good thing; it allows me to brace myself for when I take off my T-shirt and turn around.

"How's the water?" I stupidly ask as I dip my toe into the scalding hot water.

"Fucking perfect."

The lower octave of his voice makes me finally look at him. Fuck, this is going to be harder than I thought. His eyes are hungry. His face is flushed. Which means I'm going to sit my happy ass on the other side of the hot tub…far away from the man, and the cock, that makes me stupid.

"Did you hear the news?" I ask.

He nods. "Flights canceled. Roads closed too."

"I figured as much," I say. "Looks like we're here for a few days."

"Looks like it."

I hate the awkward silence that now lives between us. The best part of Grayson and I, and why I was so excited to explore whatever this was between us, was the banter. How we could make each other laugh. How topics flowed freely, and it was as easy as breathing.

Now I feel suffocated. But I need to push through it. If my friend-zone plan is going to work, we need to get over the awkward. Start now.

"I didn't know where you were when I got back to the room," I say. My topic of conversation is fine enough, but does he really have to be sitting, arms spread wide, with his hair wet? He'd really help me out right now if he just said something that was a screaming red flag. Crypto. Showing me fishing pictures. Mansplaining literally anything. I'll take a crumb at this point.

"A soak sounded nice," he says. "Since this is now my vacation, I figured I'd make the most of it."

"I figured it was because you had a crick in the neck from the cot."

He laughs. "Well, that too."

"I'll take it tonight," I offer up. "No reason for you to be the only one to suffer."

"No," he protests. "It's your room. You're not sleeping on the cot."

"I insist." I pause for a second, trying to figure out what I want to say next. I definitely want to get away from bed talk. "You're stuck here instead of going home. The least I can do is give you a real bed to sleep on."

He laughs. "Strangely enough, if I had to pick between the cot or two days of family time, the cot wins hands down."

That takes me by surprise. "That bad?"

He shakes his head as he repositions himself in the hot tub. I should get a medal for not staring at his defined chest while he does it.

"My family is…complicated."

"How so?"

I don't know if prying into personal family stories is the move here, but at least the silence isn't deafening, and for now, I'm not picturing myself sitting on his lap.

"I'm the black sheep of the family. Makes the holidays a little uncomfortable."

"Black sheep? Wait, did you leave your small town in Connecticut and the family's Christmas tree farm for the big city and the big corporate job? Because if you did, I saw a movie about that once."

The joke does its job of breaking the tension. "I saw it too. But unfortunately, that's not the one I star in."

I want him to finish telling me the story, but I need to rewind back.

"You watch cheesy Christmas movies?"

"Of course," he says. "Well, except for the ones with that one actress. What's her name…"

I know it, but I refuse to say it. "I know who you're talking about. Fuck her."

"Exactly."

We share a laugh and a smile, because that's all we know how to do, even when I'm trying to do the exact opposite. I hate that the conversation is so effortless. That we go from complicated families to cheesy television movies and bad-take actresses without skipping a beat.

This. This is what I always wanted in a partner. A guy who I could talk to like a best friend. A friend who I just so happen to want to rip his clothes off. Someone who matches my vibe while also making me yearn for them when they aren't around.

Too bad I found it in the guy I can't let myself have.

"I fell in love with public relations and media when I was in high school," he says. "I don't even remember where I read about it, or what piqued my interest, but once I discovered it, I knew that's what I wanted to do."

"And being a six-figure publicist isn't good enough for your family? Remind me to call my mom and thank her for not batting an eyelash at my career choice."

I meant it as a joke, but he doesn't laugh. "I didn't follow in the family footsteps. So because I don't have a 'JD' at the end of my name, I am forever the outcast."

"A family full of lawyers? How many are we talking here?"

"Currently practicing? Seven. A few are still in college. Another four retired, who at one time practiced under the flag."

"And then there's you."

He nods. "And then there's me, putting out statements that it wasn't my client who flashed her boobs on the roof patio before trying to fight a bachelorette."

"I remember that story!" I say. "I didn't know it was you behind the PR. You handled it beautifully."

"Thanks," he says. "Once I got her to get her story straight, that is."

I laugh, and can relate. "But she did it, right? She did the flashing and the fighting?"

He nods and lets out a laugh. "Oh, she did it. She very much did it."

"See, I think that's more impressive than being a lawyer. Sure you have to pass a few tests and know when to scream words like 'objection!' at the right time, but it takes a special skill to be able to get a diva to admit her wrongdoings, without really admitting it, and apologizing in just a way that seems sincere even though she was rolling her eyes while you were writing it for her."

Grayson's smile is so pure it hits me square in my heart. "You get it."

"Comes with the job."

The silence is back, but the awkwardness is gone. Thank goodness. Except replacing that is the overwhelming desire to float to his side of the hot tub, sit between his legs, and let him hold me tight as we lose all sense of time.

How did I think this was a good idea? Trying to get him out of my system by putting him in the friend zone was great in theory, but the execution is clearly failing. Though what did I expect? That one night of small talk was going to make me not like him anymore? That just separating myself from him wasn't going to make me want him? For a smart woman, sometimes I'm dumb as hell.

I need to leave. Get out of here while I still can. Before I do something stupid like kiss him.

"I'm going to get going," I say as I move off the wall where the jet was hitting my lower back just right.

"You just got here."

"I know," I quickly say as I stand up. "But this way I'll get in and out of the shower first, so you can have the bathroom. And I haven't eaten. Stomach is growling. You know how that goes. It's just…ACK!"

This is what I get for trying to move quickly in a tub full of water. Because one minute I'm standing up, talking a mile a minute and trying to make my exit, and then the next I'm losing my footing and about to fall back, ass first, into the water. My arms are flailing. I can't seem to get my balance. And just when I think I'm about to make a Shamu-level splash, I feel arms under me, stopping me from my fall.

"Easy there, Vixen," Grayson says, holding me still as I catch my breath. "I got you."

Dammit, he does. He really does. In so many ways.

Gradually he lifts me up, and I slowly turn around to face him. He doesn't move his hands from my arms, which could be passed off for him making sure that I have my balance. Secretly, and selfishly, I hope it's not.

I hope it's because he wants to touch me. Because I want him to. More than that, I want to kiss him. I want him to kiss me. It could happen so easily right now. We're inches away from each other. Our chests are touching, and I can feel every breath he takes. Our eyes are saying the same things.

We want this. We want each other. We want this moment—right here, right now.

God, I want to give in. I want to say fuck my rules and fuck every wall I've built over the years to protect myself.

But I don't. I can't. I know what will happen when this goes bad. When our careers get in the way. That heartbreak will be worse then than it will be now.

Which is why I do the one thing my body is screaming at me not to do—I get out of the hot tub, and I walk away.

13
grayson

I don't run after her.

I should. I want to. But I don't.

No, chasing after her will only freak her out even more. She needs time to process. To come down off the realization that we were two seconds away from kissing.

Frankly, so do I.

I wasn't prepared for Kat to be here. I thought coming down for a soak would be good for me, allow me to relax a little after today, and also give Kat the room to herself, especially when I got the alert that we were snowed in. I never suspected that she'd have the same idea, let alone share the space with me.

I wanted to bring her into my arms. Hold her. Feel her head on my chest as we sat back and relaxed. But I gave her space. I sat on my hands. My dick behaved. Everything was going fine and dandy until I watched in slow motion as she started falling back. I had no choice but to catch her, but I also knew the second she was in my arms that all bets were off.

Because it was in that second I realized that no matter what I thought of this woman before I met her, what I think of her now outweighs all of that.

She's it for me. Full stop.

Sure, she might be my competition, but when you find the woman you know could change you for the better—who sees you in a way that no other person has seen you before—you don't throw it away. You don't act like a hard-headed jackass and let something like your job, or the fact that you created a narrative in your head that she was your arch enemy, stand in your way of something special.

Which is what I now need to prove to her. Though for me, it was just an idea I needed to get over. For her? I think not mixing business with pleasure is more than a mantra—it's her rule of life. That it's rooted in history and also comes with a deep side of pain. Which means I need to show her why this can be different. Why I can be different. Help her break down those walls.

Because this? What we share? What's been evident from that first night? It's undeniable.

The problem is, I don't even know where to start when it comes to knocking down those walls. I rack my brain as I get out of the hot tub and dry myself off. For some reason, the first thing I think of is to order room service. Why? Who the hell knows. I mean, my stomach was grumbling, and she did say that she was hungry when she was trying to make a beeline out of the hot tub. I'm not sure if that was real or an excuse, but I don't think it's ever a bad move to order food.

But after that, I've got nothing. I sit and stare at the concrete surrounding the hotel pool for at least ten minutes with not a single idea. I'm willing to play the long game, but I have a feeling once the holidays are over, and we're free from Timberline Inn, Kat is going to be doing her darndest to stay away from me. Which is why I have to make my move here. I don't know how long I have, but I need to make every minute, every interaction, count.

When I get back to the room and open the door, I see that the bathroom door is shut, but I don't hear the water running. In fact, I don't hear anything, despite it being only a little after seven. When I come down the short hallway and turn toward the bed, that's when I see it.

Kat, pretending to sleep on the cot.

It's fucking adorable.

"What are you doing?" She doesn't move, and I can only laugh. "Kat, I know you're awake."

I stand over her, arms crossed in amusement, as she slowly rolls over, pretending to wake up, big yawn included. "What are you talking about? I was asleep."

"Bullshit."

"How do you know?"

I quirk an eyebrow. "Do you really want me to tell you?"

"Yes," she says, now sitting up, acting surprised by my answer. "Enlighten me."

"Because you do this cute little snore when you're sleeping, and you weren't doing that."

"I—" she cuts herself off, not able to find the words. "I don't snore."

"You do, and it's endearing," I say, not worrying about hiding my words. Not when I'm staring down a mountain that I need to climb. "Now what were you doing on the cot?"

"Sleeping," she defends again. "Well, trying to sleep."

"And why were you doing it on the cot and not the bed?"

"I told you; I'm going to be nice and sleep on it tonight," she says. "It's only fair."

I shake my head. "Absolutely not. This is your room. You're sleeping on the bed."

I mean, I'd rather us both sleep on the bed. But I know that option isn't on the table.

Yet. I'm an optimistic man.

"I'm not moving," she says, crossing her fingers and adjusting her legs to sit crisscross-applesauce. "I've already washed my face and brushed my teeth. I haven't had a sip of water today, which I know isn't something to brag about, but that means I'm not going to need to go to the bathroom for hours. There's nothing that's going to move me off this cot."

"What about food?" I ask. "You said you haven't eaten."

She shakes her head. "I'm fine. Wasn't actually that hungry. And if I want something, I can get it myself. I'm pretty independent that way."

Oh, this is how she's going to play it. This I can work with. "Oh. So you won't want any of the food I ordered?"

This throws her. "You ordered food?"

I really want to give me from thirty minutes ago a big old pat on the back.

"I did," I say as I check the time. "It's going to be here in five minutes or so."

Her eyes are about to pop out of her head. She really thought I was bluffing. "What did you order? I mean, probably won't even like it, but you know, for my information."

Now I just smile, because I know my play. Katherine might still be a bit of a mystery to me, but Kat I already know like the back of my hand. "Turns out the Timberline's room service has a good selection of comfort food."

As if on cue, there's a knock at the hotel door. "Wait here. I'm going to go get the food, and you can decide if you want to die on this hill or not."

She's silent except for a "humpf" as I answer the door and wheel in the huge tray of assorted foods. When I'm back in the room, Kat's still in the same position, only now she's staring at me as I walk past her, situating the cart against the desk, well past her arm's reach if she stays on that damn cot.

"Not that I'm hungry or anything," she says over her growling stomach. "But what toppings did you get?"

"Pizza with pepperoni and mushrooms," I say. "Someone once told me it was the elite combination."

Her stomach growls some more, and I can't help but smile the way I imagine a cartoon villain does. If I had a mustache I'd twirl it.

"I also got a little something of everything. Chicken tenders. Spinach and artichoke dip. Truffle fries. And…oh, there it is. Two slices of cheesecake."

I actually see her lick her lips, which I'm not sure she realizes she did.

"All sounds good," she says as I open the containers, letting the aroma of the food fill the room.

She holds her ground firm, which I expected. But I'm not worried. She's only going to be able to resist so long.

"This is really good," I say, taking a big scoop of the dip with a piece of pita bread. "You should try it."

"I'm good." Except I can see her eyeing the table. At any point she could ask me for a plate, but I know she won't. And I'm not going to offer either. Is this the move? I'm not sure. But like any trip to Vegas, I'm playing the hand I'm dealt. Even if it's a less than ideal one.

"Suit yourself," I say as I grab the remote, a beer from the mini fridge, and sit myself against the headboard of the bed. "I wonder what channel we can find a cheesy Christmas movie on? I haven't played my Christmas movie drinking game in forever."

This gets her attention away from the pizza. "Drinking game?"

"Of course," I say. "Every time they say Christmas, take a drink. If it's a second-chance story, take two drinks. There are a lot more where those came from, but that's the gist."

When I say forever, I mean never. I'm making this shit up as I go. Because desperate times call for desperate measures. And sometimes that comes in the form of beer and the big city girl falling for the guy who owns the Christmas tree farm.

She doesn't say anything, but I can see the wheels turning in her head. I search the channels until I see exactly what I'm looking for. "Oh, this is a good one. She's the daughter of Nicholas Saint, and he's the lawyer trying to buy the town."

Kat turns to the television, and just for a second, I think I see her smile. I don't say anything—I don't want to spook her—but I do hold my breath when I see her slowly get up from the cot and walk to where I put the food.

I slowly sit back against the headboard and watch as she takes a little bit of everything—including two slices of pizza, which I had a feeling would be her downfall—before grabbing a beer for herself and sitting next to me on the bed.

"Just because I moved doesn't mean I'm sleeping here."

"You keep telling yourself that."

She peers at me. "You say I'm stubborn, but you're not too far behind."

"What can I say?" I pause my statement to take a big bite of pizza before talking with my mouth full. "I yam who I yam."

For the first time since I got to the room, I see her relax. See her true smile. And I don't know if I've knocked down a wall yet, but I think I loosened a few bricks.

———

"Really? The store's manager is named Rudolph? You've got to be fucking kidding me."

Kat laughs through the sip of beer she's taking, because in my game, that I'm making up as I go, anytime someone has a "random" holiday-themed name, you have to take a sip.

We've taken a lot of sips.

"I mean, it fits," Kat continues as we watch the movie featuring the Christmas queen herself, Hollie Berry. "Did you know Rudolph is actually Hollie Berry's married name?"

I nearly spit my beer out. "What? No way. Also, how the hell do you know this?"

Kat sets her beer down and sits up a little straighter. "So, Hollie is married to this guy named Trent Rudolph, who lives in a tiny town about an hour south of Nashville. It's the hometown of Logan's wife, so I get to hear all the lore. I also saw her one night in the local bar. She's a lovely woman."

I don't know if I'm drunk or if she just dropped a lot of information on me. "You're making that up."

"Hand to God," she says. "It's also the town that Hazel lives in, and her husband is best friends with this Trent Rudolph."

"What kind of small-town, six degrees of separation, world are we living in?"

"The one where the town of Rolling Hills, Tennessee, is a little too busy for its population."

"Fascinating."

"It really is," she continues. "I had my doubts about moving to Tennessee when Logan told me that we were relocating to Nashville. But I've enjoyed it so far."

"Were you originally from Los Angeles?"

"No, but from California," she says, turning so she's now lying on her shoulder, facing me. "My parents still live there."

"You're not going West for the holidays?"

She shakes her head. "Parents are divorced. Dad has a new family that doesn't like me too much. You know, daughter from the 'other' family and all. I would've visited Mom, but she joined a smutty book club for divorced women over fifty and they all decided to go on a cruise for the holidays."

"Good for her."

"That's what I said. Which is why I can now go lay on a beach for a week, guilt free. Well, maybe, if it ever stops snowing."

On our second beer and second movie of the night, we decided to open the curtains to watch the snow fall. We figured if we're stuck here for it, we might as well enjoy the ambiance. And just from what I've seen, we're not leaving this hotel for a few days.

"That sounds amazing," I say. "Soon you'll be eating at a beachside restaurant with a mai tai while I'll be listening to my father brag about my brother's latest case."

"Will it at least be an interesting case?"

"Not even a little bit. He's a divorce lawyer. The best I can hope for is a torrid affair."

"I'll cross my fingers for you."

"Thanks."

The conversation fades away naturally, and we both turn our attention back to the movie. Well, partially. I can't help but notice that Kat is still turned toward me. And even more, she's now burying herself a little lower into the pillows, like she's about to go to sleep.

"You okay?"

She nods, but lets out a big yawn. "Great."

I chuckle as I check the time. I don't know when it got to be past eleven, but somehow we've drank a six-pack of beer and watched three and a half Christmas movies. "I can turn the lights off if you want to go to sleep."

At the word "sleep," her eyes flew open. *Rookie move, Ross. Damn.* She throws back the blankets and begins to rise.

"Where do you think you're going?" I ask as I pull her back down to the bed.

"To the cot."

"No, you aren't."

She wiggles out of my loose hold as she stands up. "Grayson, I appreciate the chivalry, but look at that cot. Now look at you. You were hanging off it last night. I don't mind."

"Well, I do."

"So what are we going to do? Both sleep in the bed? Is this where our stubbornness is taking us?"

I don't know if she realizes what she just suggested, but she does after the grin forms on my face.

"Actually, yes it is." I roll off the bed before heading into the closet to grab every spare pillow and blanket I can find. I even take the extra one that was being used on the cot.

"What are you doing?"

"Neither of us are going to concede." I throw the pillows on the bed, but turn so I'm now standing in front of her, a position we've found ourselves in a few times this weekend. "I'm also going to assume that I can't kiss you?"

That takes her by surprise. "Uh—no…"

"You sure?"

Her head is nodding, but the big eyes and the frog she just swallowed suggest otherwise.

"Okay then." I do kiss her forehead though. One, because I can, and two, because she's not expecting it. "Then I'm going to take these pillows, and we're going to make two beds."

She shakes her head to bring her back to reality. "A pillow fort? Are we eight?"

I level a look at her. "Do you have a better idea? I mean, we could go without, sleep in the same bed. Or, I can sleep on the cot. The choice is yours, Vixen."

She scrunches her nose at me, but I don't know if it's for the use of the name or the options I laid out for her. I just like that I'm getting a reaction of any kind.

"I'm going to guess that no decision means we're sharing a bed," I say, putting the last of the pillows on the bed. "Now, I'm going to pop into the bathroom quickly. That okay?"

She nods. "Yeah. You go first."

I move quickly, brushing my teeth and washing my face before slipping on a T-shirt and pajama pants. If I was fucking with her, I'd choose to sleep shirtless tonight—yes, I noticed how she looked at me in the hot tub today. Yes, it made me feel really fucking good—but the fact that I'm sleeping with her at all is the win I'm going to take. No sense in being greedy.

Kat and I silently switch places, and while she's in the bathroom, I clean up the space, putting the empty food containers out in the hallway to get picked up and also grab my book and reading glasses from the desk. I make myself comfortable on the left side of the bed, propped up on the headboard once more, which is where I'm sitting when she comes out.

"What are you doing?" she asks.

I look around, because I'm not sure if I'm missing something. "Reading?"

"No." She points to me, then jerks her thumb to the other side. "That's my side."

"But this is the side I was sitting at all night."

"Yeah, and that was fine for TV watching. Now it's time for sleeping, and I sleep on the left side."

I shake my head. "No can do."

"But—"

"But what, Kat?"

I fight off my smile, because I can tell she's tongue-tied. I love it when I do that to her. "When…the last time we—"

"Slept together?"

"Yes. The last time we slept together," she says in a huff, finally taking a few steps toward the bed. "I distinctly remember you being on the right side of the bed, which was great, because that's not my side of the bed. But here you are, being on my side. So I'm going to need you to switch."

I look to my right then back to her. "Nope. Sorry. Get comfy, roomie. It's time for bed. Either that or the cot."

It's a bold move I just made, but I know for a fact how uncomfortable that thing is. If she chooses that over the bed, she's more stubborn than I thought.

"Listen, Grayson, I'm honestly a pretty go-with-the-flow person. But there are a few things in my life that I need to happen. It always has to be Heinz Ketchup. Twizzlers over Red Vines. And I have to sleep on the left side of the bed."

"Yeah…no," I say, putting down my book and flipping off the light on my side.

"No?" she squawks, even though she does walk to *her* side of the bed and gets in. "Why are you being so difficult? What happened to the chivalry?"

I wait for her to fully lie down before I roll over the pillow fort, hovering on top of her. My move catches her by surprise, her brown eyes round and unblinking. And it takes all, and I mean all, the power in my body to not lean down and take those perfect lips with mine.

"I sleep closest to the door," I begin. "That's why I slept on the other side last time, and it's why I'm going to sleep here now. This is a non-negotiable, Kat. Because I am chivalrous. Also, if we were walking, I'd be on the side closest to the street. I'll always open a car door for you. Hold open a door. And always, I mean always, will I be the one sleeping closest to the door. Do you understand?"

Kat is silent, just nodding at my words. I take advantage of the situation, and lean down, gently pressing a kiss to her forehead.

Another bold move? Absolutely. But frankly, I don't know when I'll be able to do it again, and I wasn't going to waste that chance.

"Oh, and one last thing," I say, lowering myself the closest I can get to her without touching. "I'm not going to kiss you. That is, until you ask me to. Because I am chivalrous. And I'm willing to wait however long it takes."

guide to christmas (and love) rule #120

Grey sweatpants and glasses should be automatic qualifiers for the naughty list.

14

kat

I'M A CHICKEN SHIT.

That and the pillow fort was as useful as a Zippo in hell.

Never in a million years did I think I'd describe myself as that. I'm pretty good at confrontation. I stand up for myself, and those I care about, when I need to. If I do something wrong, I fess up to it. All in all, I've never been one to back down or run away.

Except, apparently, when I wake up on the chest of the man I shouldn't be waking up on. Then I turn into a big old wussy and sprint from the hotel room like I just egged someone's house.

Thanks for nothing, pillow fort…

When I started to wake up, I knew before even opening my eyes that I felt more refreshed than I had in days. Part of it was from the hot tub and my muscles being relaxed. But then I felt Grayson's arms around me. His firm chest underneath me. That's when I really knew why I slept like a baby. Because I felt safe. Protected. I had a man who went **toe-to-toe** with me to sleep on the side of the bed closest to a door in case of a hypothetical intruder.

Dammit…I'm all sorts of fucked.

Once I realized where I was, I didn't move for more than a

few minutes. And not because I was comfortable and warm and cozy—really, it wasn't because of that. It was because I didn't know how to get out of his hold without waking him up. Because I couldn't be here when he opened his eyes. I couldn't have the awkward morning talk. We didn't have it that first night, and I loved it. It was part of the reason I knew I wanted to see him again. I hated yesterday, when we had our bouts of silence where no one knew what to say. And for a woman who is known for her crisis management skills, it's baffling that I don't know how to handle this situation. More specifically, these feelings.

I want him. I like him. I really, really, like him. Maybe more than anyone I've ever tried to date, or even considered in that avenue. Every time I see him, I want to kiss him. I didn't want to leave a bed today, because being next to him was the best feeling in the world.

Which also made it be the worst feeling in the world. I can't date him. I can't be with him. I know it's not fair to judge him against past experiences, but I don't see a way our careers can coexist within a relationship. So why go into something when you know how it's gonna end? Especially when that ending is heartbreak.

So I got out of there. I stepped on pillows, almost tripped over the cot, poked my eye out when I put my contact lens in, but eventually, made it to the restaurant.

I'm shocked to even find a table. I think every guest is here, which isn't surprising since we're all pretty much stuck and this is one of our only options for food. Luckily, the waitress is on her game. and I order almost immediately. As she brings over my coffee and apple juice, I fire up the laptop to check some emails. Might as well. since the vacation isn't happening.

On first glance, there's nothing out of the ordinary. Emails from GameTech that I'm always included on as part of the senior leadership team. A few specifically from Logan, asking me to look into a few things—though he did qualify his request by saying that I'm not to do a thing until after January 1. When I switch over to my freelance Katherine email, I'm pleased to see three asking if I'm taking on new clients. But most importantly, I'm not seeing the "thanks but no thanks" email from Declan and Howard. Granted, I doubt they made their decision on a day when their hotel got busier than they probably expected because of the snow. It would also be a little sticky if they let either Grayson or I down when we're both staying here for the foreseeable future.

My breakfast comes out quicker than I expected for how busy the restaurant is, and I start doing a morning doom scroll while I eat my eggs and turkey sausage. I'm six videos in to an "Am I The Asshole?" story when movement catches my eye.

I knew he'd be down sooner rather than later. It's not like we have food in our room. And while this hotel is pretty big, it's really small when you're snowed in.

Fuck...why is he so fucking hot? It's actually unfair, especially because the clothes he's wearing now are so casual it's criminal. He's in a white T-shirt with a coordinating gray zip-up hoodie and *joggers*. And he's wearing his glasses.

Gray sweatpants and glasses? He might as well have a sign above his head that says "Yes, I'm dressed like a whore. Any problems with that?"

The answer is no. There are no problems. And I'm not the only one thinking that. Every woman he walks by is looking at him. I think I saw one actually lick her lips. Another was holding her baby, with her husband next to her, and I watched in real time as her jaw dropped. Hell, I think the baby's did too.

But he didn't see any of that. Because that whole time, he was only looking at me.

Son of a bitch, I'm so screwed...

"Good morning," he says as he stands next to my table. "Up early today?"

I try to decipher if he knows that I snuck out or if he truly did sleep through it. Damn his poker face. "Yeah, and I didn't want to wake you. Figured I'd come down and get some work done. Wait, what is that?"

I don't know how I didn't notice that this whole time Grayson's holding two cups of coffee in a carrier—one hot, one iced.

"One for you, and one for me," he says as he sets down the container. "I had a feeling both of us would be working today— because it's what workaholics do when they're snowed-in and can't start their mandated vacations. And I know working without coffee is criminal, so I thought I'd bring you one. Apologies if I messed up the flavors. I went with the Christmas special. In my opinion, you can't go wrong with peppermint and mocha."

I'm nearly speechless as I stare at the drink. "Thank you."

Iced coffee, slutty glasses, and gray sweatpants? This is my Sunday morning, lazy-girl fantasy come true. Because this is what I imagine it would be like. Okay, not at a hotel. But Grayson and me. Sitting on a couch. Sipping our drinks. Comfy clothes. If it could all just be this simple…

"You're welcome." He looks around in the dining room. "Do you mind if I sit here? Maybe share the table as we get some work done? I think this might be the only open seat in the hotel."

And there's the crash. The vision of lazy Sunday mornings ruined by the thought of us working on the couch together and him just happening to look to see what I'm working on. Or small talk that seems innocuous but is really picking my brain. Next thing I know, every idea I've ever had is being pitched by someone other than me, and I'm watching my ideas get promoted while I'm left confused and heartbroken.

Grayson can see the panicked look on my face. I hate that my breathing is picking up. I feel ridiculous. I shouldn't have this kind of reaction to something that happened eight years ago. But I do. Because that's how emotional trauma works.

"Hey," he says, setting down his bag and crouching down to

be at my eye level. "I don't have to. I can find somewhere else to go."

I look up at him, and his eyes...his voice...they're so sincere. He's rubbing his thumb over my wrist, trying to help me calm down.

I shake my head as I even my breathing. I *do* want him to. I enjoy his company. I can't lie to myself about that anymore. "No. I want you to. It's just..."

I trail off, not ready to tell him about my past. I don't know if I'll ever be, but I should give him some reason why my face is whiter than the snow outside.

"How about we start with breakfast? Then we'll take our computers out. I'll stay on my side of the table. That's all that has to happen. Sound like a plan?"

I nod. "I like that."

"Good." He starts moving closer to me, and for a second I think he's gonna kiss my forehead. I hold my breath, hoping that's what he's going to do. Why? Because I'm selfish and apparently a glutton for punishment.

Except he doesn't. Instead of feeling his lips against me, he taps his forehead to mine.

"This goes as slow as you want," he says. "Just know that whenever you're ready for the next move, I'll be here, waiting to do it with you."

I blink a few times as I process his words. Sure, he could be talking about this actual interaction. Me and him having a workday together.

But no...it means more. So much more.

The question now is, when will I be ready for that next move come? If ever?

———

"Craziest thing you've done for a client?"

I think about his question, but frankly it's not even a competition. "The craziest thing I personally had to do for a client was bake and deliver twenty-dozen cookies to the editor of a magazine because a client wanted to be on a list of fifty powerful people or some shit like that. The crazy part was, this wasn't my client."

Grayson's reaction—confused but wanting to know more—is fitting for this story. "Please continue. I'm intrigued."

"As you should be," I say with an eyebrow wag. "I bought cookies for an office potluck day because I don't bake. I barely cook. Anyway, I joked that of course I got up at the crack of dawn to bake them, because I'm sarcastic and that's what I do."

"Naturally."

"Anyway, the client in question, a movie director, happened to be in the office that day and grabbed a few. He loved them. Thought they were the best thing he ever tasted. Someone who didn't sense the sarcasm told him that I baked them myself. And I don't know what got it into his head, but he was convinced that if I, a little ol' junior account manager whose name he didn't know, were to bake and deliver these cookies to the keeper of this list, that he'd get on. So on the instructions of my boss and my boss's boss, I did it. I believe they equated it to 'taking one for the team.'"

"Wow," Grayson says in disbelief. "Did he get on the list?"

"Absolutely not," I say with a laugh. "He was a shitty director making shitty movies. No cookies can fix that. Though the magazine that published the list did appreciate the effort, and I did a few campaigns with them after that, so it all worked out."

"Hell, yeah," Grayson says, tipping his now lukewarm coffee cup to me. "I once had to pay off a pizza delivery guy who accidentally walked in on my client hosting an orgy."

I spit out my water. "Excuse me? Did you just say what I think you just said?"

"I did. No one was answering the door, and he heard music around back, so he walked around to deliver it. In his defense, the instructions did say 'hand to customer,' and he was doing his job. He just didn't realize why no one's hands were free."

"Holy shit," I say. "I know you can't tell me, but I really want to know who this was."

Grayson shakes his head. "Bound by an NDA and my personal code of ethics, which include no outright lying, no blabbing, and certainly no cheating."

The no-cheating one sticks with me. "You realize now I'm just going to dig to figure out who it was."

"I'd expect nothing less."

This has been how the conversation has gone. A little work, a little chat, shared smiles, a lot of laughs. Pretty much the perfect day.

It was almost inevitable that the conversation would turn to our jobs. But in a shocking turn of events for me, I'm glad it has. It's been superficial talk. Random campaigns we've worked on. Biggest flops. Biggest wins. Nothing too technical. Just enough to get me comfortable with this line of conversation. It's like he knows exactly what I needed.

Of course he does. He has since the moment I met him.

"I don't know, son… If these two are here any longer, we might need to give them resident status."

Grayson and I both look up to see Howard and Declan walking up to our table, each dressed as if Christmas is happening right now.

"I must say, I do appreciate you going all-in on the Santa persona right now," I say to Howard. "The red cardigan suits you."

"This old thing?" he says, but he does add a little bit of modeling for me. "Just dusting it off for our Christmas party tonight."

"Christmas party?" Grayson asks. "Is this your employee Christmas party?"

"The opposite," Declan says. "We're hosting one for all the guests. And we wanted to personally invite you both."

"What kind of party are we talking here?" I ask. "You know, so I know what to wear."

"A very impromptu one, but one that includes champagne, hors d'oeuvres, and music, so dress in whatever makes you feel that mood," Howard says. "We know this weather is less than ideal for the guests who, like you, are stranded here, or the ones who had to make unscheduled pit stops to get off the roads. We thought by throwing a party tonight, it would lessen the load."

"Great idea," Grayson says. "And something like that helps the goodwill of the guests. They might be grumpy now, but knowing you're doing this, especially if it's at no cost to them, that's PR you can't manufacture."

"We weren't thinking about that, but that's wonderful," Declan says. "Though actually, this idea spawned from PR."

"How so?" I ask.

"You," Howard says. "We got the idea after our meeting yesterday."

Shit, what did I say? I say a lot of things in a pitch, so who knows what landed and what didn't. I also try to sneak a peek to Grayson to see his reaction, but without making it obvious, I can't get a read. "I'm glad I was able to give you an idea."

"That's the funny thing, you didn't say anything specific," Howard says. "But, when you talked about activities and things to do around the hotel, it...I don't know, it just got our brains working."

"We're going to have a play area for the children, fully staffed to look after them, so parents can have some Christmas fun before the big day gets here. We also have some teens, so we're going to have a space set aside for them," Declan explains. "Then, of course, the party for the adults. Because what is a good Christmas party without some reindeer games?"

"Reindeer games, you say?"

I don't know why I'm so surprised, but Grayson's demeanor toward Declan is now...nice? Happy? I mean, it should've been the whole time. But gone is the man who was trying to shoot daggers at him via his eyes, and here is an enthusiastic about-to-be party participant. I wonder what changed?

"I do say," Declan says. "And don't worry, Christmas trivia is a part of that."

Grayson laughs. "Then I'll be there with jingle bells on."

I feel like I missed six chapters of a book. But before I can ask about anything, Declan and Howard are saying their goodbyes, while reminding us that festivities start at seven tonight.

It's quiet for a few beats before Grayson speaks up first. "I'm going to ask the question, but you can tell me to fuck off."

That makes me laugh, but it's a nervous laugh, because I have a feeling what it's going to be about. "With an opener like that, how can I not at least hear it?"

He leans forward, clasping his hands together. "What did you say to Declan and Howard? What made them suddenly want to do this party?"

He told me I could tell him to fuck off. That I didn't have to answer. And my gut reaction is to not, especially considering what I said was nothing groundbreaking, and it's also why I think I'm so successful in picking up clients. This is what Grayson's wanted—he wants to know how I win.

And I want to tell him. Maybe this is the test. See how he reacts. If I'm even considering pursuing this—and right now that's still an if—this is a hurdle we have to cross. Might as well jump it now, while it's there for the taking.

Look at me...one small step for man, one big step for conquering emotional damage.

"I've found that my best presentations have nothing to do with telling them specific things to do. Making a client feel like they came up with the idea, but with a little help from me, seems to go a long way."

Grayson seems baffled. "Are you kidding me? No specifics?"

"A few," I say. "I can't make it look like I come in unprepared. But I make sure the ideas I do bring in are broad, that way it gives them a chance for their brains to work as well. And that's what I did here. I mentioned excursions for adults and kids, and having services set up for parents so if they wanted to go out on their own, they have childcare covered. Give them a resort feel without the resort prices. That's what they can market on. That's what will bring in young families who want to travel with children, but also feel like they're younger adults having memory-making experiences as well."

"Fuck…" Grayson says, shaking his head. "That's brilliant. If I had ideas like that maybe I'd have moved up the corporate ladder faster."

"Is that what you want? A corner office at Sterling Strategies?"

He nods. "That's been the goal. To become the youngest senior account executive in the company's history. If I do it within the next eighteen months, I'll hit the record."

"It's a good goal to have," I say. "But what I threw out? Don't beat yourself up about it. It was just an idea. I mean, I didn't bring up podcasters. Putting them on a national stage? That was smart. Senior account executive smart."

"Thanks," Grayson says, a little blush hitting his cheeks. "Wait. How did you know I did that?"

"Because that was one thing I didn't have in my presentation that you did, and they specifically asked me what my ideas were in that space. I had to scramble. You threw me for a loop, Ross."

I can tell he's trying to hold back a smile, but I want him to have this moment.

"You can smile," I say. "Point for Grayson."

"Thank you. But I should also award you a point. You're a worthy foe."

"As are you."

"Can I ask you a question now?"

He nods. "Shoot."

"How did he know about Christmas trivia?"

I watch as Grayson's cheeks blush. I wasn't expecting that reaction.

"Declan asked how we met. I told him you were the best trivia partner I could've asked for. That when we teamed up, no one else stood a chance."

The smiles we're sharing right now are unlike any moment I've ever had with anyone. I don't have a single fear that he's going to steal anything we just talked about. I don't feel like he's been mentally taking notes today of how to finally beat me. No, this look here is only filled with admiration. Respect. And dare I say…no. It can't be that.

But it is making me think of some scary things.

Maybe I can do this.

Maybe *we* can do this.

And, the scariest of all, how badly I *want* to do this.

guide to christmas (and love) rule #45

Some kisses outrank others. Ones under the mistletoe are in a category by themselves.

15

kat

Do I wear it?

That's the question I've been asking myself for no less than the last twenty minutes as I get ready for tonight's party. Because I want to be bold. I want to take a chance. I want to do a lot of things, and wearing the outfit I want to wear would give me that extra ounce of confidence.

But then there's fucking Katherine in the back of my head, asking me if that's a good idea.

Sometimes she's a stuck-up bitch.

The outfit Katherine wants me to wear is a flattering, and slightly sexy, red sweater with leather leggings. Just enough to give party vibes, but appropriate for a function being hosted by potential clients.

But what I *want* to wear is a Santa Baby inspired dress made of dark green velvet, with the fur hood and all. I packed it for a just-in-case moment, because when you're gone over the holiday for ten days, you never know what you're going to need. I bought it a few years ago for a Bad Santa Christmas party, and frankly, I look way too good in it to only wear it once. It makes me feel sexy. Bold. Not like Katherine in the least bit.

That's who I want to be tonight. I want to be Kat. I want to be the woman who has fun. I want to be the woman who does the scary thing. And there's nothing scarier than telling a man you know could break your heart that you want to give it a try.

How's that going to happen tonight? No clue. I'm normally a pretty prepared person, but I'm winging this shit. I've only said a few words to Grayson since he made his way up to the room after our impromptu work date today, and those were "I'll pop into the bathroom now so you can have it to get ready." Not exactly the starter to the conversation of "Hey, I'm scared to death, and I need to tell you about my emotional baggage, but if you want to date, I want to date." Granted, I don't know what actually is the starter to that conversation, but I doubt it's that.

All I do know is that when I left the restaurant today, and after spending the afternoon with Grayson, I realized that I'm tired of splitting my personalities. I'm tired of needing to rely on a name and a beige bra to keep my heart protected. I don't want to live a life of regrets, and I have a feeling if I don't give this a shot with Grayson, then regret is all I'm going to feel.

And in this outfit? With a red lip, black heels, and a dress that makes me feel like I can own a room? There's no space for regret.

When I open the door, I'm hit with the smell of Grayson's cologne. The only problem is he's nowhere to be found.

I let out a sigh of disappointment as I walk over to the desk chair, so I can finish putting on my jewelry. But when I sit down, a piece of paper catches my eye.

> KATHERINE,
> CAN YOU ASK KAT TO MEET ME DOWNSTAIRS FOR A DRINK BEFORE THE PARTY? I'D LOVE TO BUY HER ONE IN CELEBRATION OF A HARD-FOUGHT BATTLE.
> LET'S HAVE SOME FUN TONIGHT.
> <3 GRAYSON

The note is simple, but I don't know if he realizes the magnitude of him writing this note to both Katherine and Kat. Does he know that I've been struggling all day of how to morph the two back together again? And even if he doesn't—which how could he—him acknowledging both of these people exist in me means more than he could ever know. Jeff never did that. Well, I take that back. He did. But he used one against the other so much that I didn't trust myself in either my professional or personal life.

But that's not Grayson. The more I spend time with him, the more I know that to be true.

I finish putting on my gold jewelry, and give myself one more spritz of perfume before I make my way downstairs. When I turn from the elevator into lobby, my eyes go wide because… damn.

Was this the same area I left just a few hours ago? There have been decorations up since I arrived, but now? I don't know when they did this, or who's responsible, but the entire space looks like you stepped into a magazine spread. Holly and lights everywhere. I don't know how they brought in more Christmas trees, but they did. Some have simple decorations. Some are currently being decked by children in their pajamas. It's absolutely perfect.

My eyes are roaming everywhere, but they stop on a dime when I look ahead and see Grayson standing outside of the restaurant.

I was not prepared.

I stop moving, and my knees nearly give out as he starts walking over to me. He's wearing black suit with a white button-down shirt. As I get closer, I realize he's wearing a Christmas tie that's just enough fun to be playful, but not take away from the sleekness of his look. His beard has the perfect amount of scruff, his hair is styled perfectly, and I can smell his cologne as he draws closer.

"You look…" He doesn't have the words. Which I get, because neither do I.

"I could say the same thing."

Neither of us are moving, both locked into this forcefield

we've fallen into. I know he's being a gentleman. His hands are balled at his sides, fists tight to keep from touching me.

And then there's me…trying to figure out how to put together the words to say that I'm here. That I want to try; I just don't know how. I know he's not going to turn me away or reject me. Between the words he's said last night and today, combined with the look of absolute yearning in his eyes, I know the answer. Yet, that doesn't make me less nervous. There's something about putting yourself out there that can scare the most confident woman into submission. Even one wearing a slutty Santa dress.

No, Kat. This is why you wore this dress. This is why you wore the black lingerie. Why the red lip is red lipping. No more being scared. No more living in the past.

I reach for his hands, wrapping his fists around my fingers. When he realizes what I'm doing, his eyes are back on me, and his smile? Instant and bright. The Christmas lights in the lobby have nothing on him right now.

"We have a lot to talk about," I say, rubbing my thumb over his knuckles. "But I have a question for you first."

"Anything."

I step a little closer, our fingers now laced together. "Since you asked me for a drink, I was wondering when that was over, if you'd be my date to a Christmas party. I have on good authority there will be trivia involved."

He laughs and pulls me in, his lips finding my forehead. I know it's not the kiss I'm craving, but God, do his lips feel good against my skin.

"I'd be honored," he says as he let's go of my hand, but only so he can put his on the small of my back. "I hear the bar makes a hell of an Old Fashioned."

"Sounds perfect."

———

"And your winners of tonight's Christmas trivia are…Claus Deep!"

I jump up from my seat, celebrating like that announcement was new information. It's not. We've been winning since round one, and frankly, when the hardest question of the night was about Linus's monologue in *A Charlie Brown Christmas*, I knew we had it in the bag.

Don't fuck with me on The Peanuts.

"Congratulations!" Declan announces on his microphone, bringing us over a prize basket. "Now, we're going to take a break from the games for a few minutes. Please, enjoy the food and desserts. And don't be afraid to turn this space into a dance floor if you so desire. Enjoy."

There's faint applause from the room, but that's not an indicator of how this night is going. Declan and Howard are nailing this. If this is what they can do with a spur-of-the-moment event, then they are going to knock Declan's vision for the Timberline out of the water.

"Well done, partner," Grayson says. "We make quite a team."

"That we do." I say as I nudge his shoulder. One that's been inches away from me all night.

I know teasing and foreplay are necessary parts of the sexual experience, but my God, this has been torture. Especially when Grayson was spending most of the night tracing small circles on my thigh. If he wasn't doing that, he had his arm around me, or was holding my hand.

But has he kissed me yet? Absolutely not. I didn't know you could actually die from anticipation, but here I am, on life support.

I mean, I probably deserve this. This is my punishment from God, Santa, and Frosty the Snowman himself for not having my head out of my ass sooner. I know the payoff is going to be worth it, but holy shit, is it payday yet?

"Are you okay if I step away for a second?" he asks.

"Of course. I actually wanted to go grab another drink and some cookies. Want me to grab you anything?"

He shakes his head before leaning into me. "One more drink. Then we're leaving. And then we're going to go upstairs so I can fuck you in that dress. And maybe those shoes. Sound good?"

Goosebumps instantly form on every inch of my body, with his words and his breath next to my ear.

"Yes."

My word is a whisper as his lips are still just centimeters from my cheek. I still, waiting to feel his lips on my cheek, but instead, he just walks away.

Bastard.

I don't know how he's going to pay for this...but once we have sex once or twenty times tonight, payback is going to be a bitch.

After I get myself back together, I make my way to the bar. I order two old fashioneds—the holiday version that Grayson and I have become fond of. I start eyeing the dessert table when I see someone slide up next to me.

"You could've given others a chance. Or maybe gotten one wrong just to make others feel better."

I laugh at Declan's joke. "Do you think either of us have that in us?"

"Not in the least."

We share a smile as the DJ, who I'm pretty sure I saw yesterday acting as a bell hop, starts playing a poppy Christmas ballad, which leads guests to taking the dance floor.

"You know if it was any other night, and you were any other person, I'd be asking you to dance right now."

That takes me by surprise. "What?"

"Don't freak out, I'm not," he says, his hands up in surrender. "Though I will admit, the first time we met, your beauty blew me away."

"Thank you?" I have no idea where this is going. I don't

think it's venturing toward inappropriate grounds, but I don't have a map, and I have a feeling this is about to be a journey.

"And then I saw how Grayson reacted to just my mere presence and one compliment. Then I knew."

Oh. Yup. The GPS didn't warn me for that turn. "You did? He did?"

This makes Declan laugh as he signals the bartender for a drink. "From the second I introduced myself, and from talking to the two of you for a minute, I realized that the 'acquainted friends' were much, much more."

"Oh," I say, feeling embarrassed. "I promise, our relationship, past and maybe present, has had no bearing on our presentations or potential business."

"Dad and I have no worries about that. You were both professional and gave us both interesting, and very different, presentations."

I let out a sigh of relief. "I'm glad to hear that."

"As I was saying, Katherine…or do you prefer Kat? That's what I heard Grayson call you."

"Oh…yeah…I go by Katherine in professional settings. Helps me keep the lines clear."

Well, it did until Grayson Ross came into my life with an eraser and told my lines to go fuck themselves.

"Let me tell you a little something about lines," Declan says. "I understand not wanting to cross them. Boundaries are put in place for a reason, and everyone has their own. But when you find the person? The one you want to blur them for? The one who makes you look at someone like Grayson looked at you that first day, and really, every day since you two have been here? You find a way to redraw them. Because that person? They only come in your life once in a lifetime. Don't let arbitrary lines get in the way of something special."

Wow. That was quite a monologue. I'm speechless, and by the time I can form a word, Grayson is back next to me, taking my hand in his.

"Can I steal my girl for a dance?"

I smile until I realize what he just said. His...his girl? When did that happen? Did I blackout after the monologue, get in a relationship with Grayson while he was in the bathroom, and I don't remember? What is it with this man and me feeling like I missed out on whole-ass conversations?

I see Declan smile at my confusion. "Absolutely. You two have fun."

I'm still slack-jawed as I abandon our drinks and trail Grayson to the dance floor. Sure, I want to dance. I want to be in his arms and feel the music run through me. But not before I get some clarification.

"Wait," I say as I pull him back toward a corner of the ballroom that's not fully private, but out of the way of the rest of the guests. "Can you clarify what you said back there?"

"What I said? You might need to be more specific."

His mischievous smile tells me he doesn't need me to repeat the question; he just wants me to.

"What you said to Declan. You called me—"

The song changes to another ballad, and before answering, Grayson pulls me into his embrace. "What I said, was that I wanted to dance with my girl. That's you, Vixen."

Okay. So I heard it correct. "Did I miss a memo about that? I haven't checked my email in a few hours."

He laughs and wraps both arms around me, holding me tight by the small of my back.

"I've known from the second I saw you in that ridiculous Christmas sweater that you could change my life. Granted, I didn't know who you were, but I knew you were someone special. And if anything has been proven over these last few days, it's that you are special. What we have is special. But more importantly, it's undeniable."

In all of the scenarios I thought about today, of how I'd tell Grayson that I want to try this, this was never how it worked out. But it's perfect. Because any lingering doubts I had, they've all been washed away.

"Yes, it is," I whisper. "But if I'm your girl, does that make you my guy?"

It sounds cheesy, but the smile on Grayson's face says he doesn't care. "Fuck, yeah, I am."

I have more to say, but I can't. Not when Grayson's mouth is on mine in a kiss that's been days in the making. How does it feel like I haven't kissed him in years? My mouth opens for him, my hands clinging to his shoulders, as he takes my mouth in his.

This. This is where I want to be. In his arms. His mouth taking what it wants. Our tongues moving in a perfect symphony.

Us. Together. A team that should be rivals, but instead are going to join forces for something neither of us can deny.

We slowly back away—I think we would've kept kissing had not someone gotten on the microphone to announce that the next game was starting—when I tilt my head toward the ceiling.

"Well, look at that," I say, signaling above our heads. "Mistletoe."

When I look back at Grayson, his smile is goofy and perfect. "Good thing I kissed you."

I wrap my arms around his neck, pulling him back in. "Is that it? Just one kiss?"

He shakes his head as he brings me back in, this kiss much tamer than our last one. "Never, Vixen. One will never be enough."

16
grayson

How I didn't drag her away from the party, sprinting through the lobby toward the elevators, I'll never know.

And frankly, I should've. The rest of the night, we were barely around each other, let alone in the vicinity where I could touch her—which is what I really wanted. I thought we had a window to make an escape, but just as I was about to pull us out of there, Howard stepped in front of us, blocking our path, insisting that we were needed for the next reindeer game. If he saw the fake excitement on our faces, he didn't react. Declan did, who was standing behind him, laughing under his breath. He knew we weren't going to say no. Between them not making their decision yet between Kat and I, and that Howard was in his formal Santa suit—beard and all—it felt wrong to deny him.

Except that the one reindeer game led to another. And another. And another. It wouldn't have been horrible, except a few were men versus women. How am I supposed to flirt and hold her hand and touch her in every acceptable way when she's across the room from me?

Then again, going head-to-head with her was pretty fun. The look of competition in her eyes? The way she bites her lip when she's concentrating? It put our situation into perspective that yes, she is my rival, but sleeping with the enemy could—and will—be a lot of fun.

That is, if I can just figure out where she's at.

The party ended about thirty minutes ago, and the guests are finally starting to make their way to their rooms. Some are carrying their sleeping children. Others are stumbling, but all smiles, as they get on the elevator. But Kat is nowhere to be found.

"Where are you?" I whisper to no one. But it's then that I see a figure standing outside on the balcony, looking like a vision under the light of the moon and the snow coming down.

"What are you doing out here?" I ask, quickly slipping off my jacket and putting it around her shoulders. "Aren't you freezing?"

I wrap her in my arms to keep her warm, though it's not as cold as I'd expect for the fact that there's ten inches of snow on the ground. That much snow where I'm from is only mildly inconvenient. But in Tennessee? This is record-setting.

"I'm better now," she says. "Sorry I disappeared. Just wanted to get some fresh air, and you were chit-chatting with Declan."

Ah, that's when she snuck out. "Yes. He found another podcast he thought I'd like. It's a historical sports one. Who knew I'd bond with a dude during a pitch about podcasts?"

"Who knew you'd bond with him about anything, after the looks you were shooting him after we arrived."

I shrug. "He's not so bad."

She turns around in my arms, quickly wrapping hers around my midsection. "That's not what you thought the first day we all met."

I laugh and squeeze her tighter. "I didn't like how he was looking at you."

"And how was he looking at me?"

I know this is payback from earlier when I made her repeat when I called her mine. "Like you were available. That he wanted you."

"But I was."

I shake my head. "Technically, yes. But that didn't mean I liked it."

She lifts up on her toes to give me a small kiss. "You know I never would've done anything with him, right?"

"I do now."

"I don't….or should I say…didn't cross that line in the business world. And that definitely included clients."

"Again, I know that now," I say. "But then? All I saw was him getting something I wasn't. It also didn't help that I just learned who you were, so I was still processing that. Actually, can we just forget how I acted that first night and chalk it up to a brief episode of douche-y rage?"

"We can," she says as she turns back around so we're both looking at the snow. "That is, if you can forgive me for my chronic stubbornness."

I lean down to press a gentle kiss behind her ear. "Am I forgiving Kat or Katherine?"

There's a shift in the air that has nothing to do with the snowfall or the wind. I pull her in tighter, wanting her to know that whatever she wants to say, I'm here for her.

"I used to work for a firm like you do. I was one of those young, excited, do whatever you ask them to do junior executives. Work sixteen-hour days. Weekends. Anything to get ahead."

"Oh, the days," I say. "Where you'd take any scrap of work they'd give you, and you treated it like it was the most important thing in the world."

"Exactly. But from the beginning, one of mid-level publicists took a liking to me. He said I had good ideas and invited me to be on his team for a huge product rollout. I was the only junior to be asked to come on board. I was so excited."

I pull her in tighter to me, having a feeling where this is going. Still, it's her story, and I'm going let her tell it, no matter how long she needs.

"He used a lot of my ideas during that time, but I didn't think anything of it. It was a collaborative effort. I was part of the team. The team got the win. I assumed that's how things went."

"Normally they do," I say. "But I'm guessing there's more?"

She nods, and I feel her hands gripping tighter onto my forearms. "After that project he asked me out. The only policy about dating in the workplace was that senior executives couldn't date subordinates. But since he wasn't in a senior leadership role yet, we were good."

Yup. I know where this is going. And I already want to kill this guy.

"It started good, just like any other relationship. Fun dates. Knowing looks across the office. Before I knew it, I had a key to his place and had all but moved out of the apartment I had with Logan."

"And knowing our business, that meant you were bringing work home with you."

"Exactly. And since we worked together, the conversations we had felt more collaborative than anything. He'd ask me what I'd do in a certain situation, or what ideas I had for a hypothetical product campaign. I answered honestly, because that's who I am, and didn't think anything of it. They weren't groundbreaking ideas, in my opinion. Because if they were, he, or someone above him, should've thought of that, you know?"

"Oh I do," I say. "I also know that just because you're higher on the food chain doesn't mean you're the smartest person in the room."

"I know that now," she says. "But then I thought I was just brainstorming ideas. Sure, he'd use a few of them, but I really didn't think anything of it. And when I'd ask him if he did use it, he'd pass it off. Make it seem like it wasn't that big of a deal. And after a while, I figured it wasn't."

"I'm guessing this hit a boiling point?"

"It did," she says, taking a deep breath before continuing. "He had the chance to pitch for a multi-million-dollar campaign.

He couldn't fuck it up. A promotion was on the line, and I knew the stress was getting to him. So every night we'd go back to his place and work on it. We thought of everything: How he was going to use his advertising dollars. Strategy. Media rollout. Press tours."

"When you say 'we' I'm guessing that meant you."

I feel her shrug against me. "I thought I was helping. It wasn't until much later that I truly realized I put together his entire presentation for him."

I've seen this happen; people taking credit for another's work is more prevalent in firms than I care to admit. But someone you care about doing it to you? That has to fucking sting.

"What happened?"

"He got the account. And the promotion." She pauses for more than a few beats, and by the way she's breathing, she might be holding back a tear. "It was a huge account for the firm, so they had this big office celebration party, champagne and all. And of course, Jeff gave a speech."

"Of course he did. Let me guess, he didn't thank you."

"I would've liked to have just been mentioned," she says. "Mind you, it wasn't a secret that we were dating. So the fact that after he thanked everyone, from his bosses, to the assistants, to legal, to graphics, and even to the food delivery person for keeping him well fed during all the late nights he put in, but not me, stung. Not once. Not a thank you. Not anything."

"Fuck, Kat. What an asshole."

"He was. And I was livid. It's one thing to use my ideas— and I know he did because he practiced his pitch speech on me the night before he gave it, and I saw the slides that I designed and put together—but to not even give me a passing 'oh, and thanks Kat,' sent me over the edge."

"You didn't go by Katherine then?"

"I did. Mostly," she says. "When I presented to clients, I was more formal. But when it came to around the office, Kat felt fine. Katherine is such a serious name. And at that point, the only person who called me that was my mom, when I was in trouble, or Logan, when he was fucking with me. Kat, I thought, made me more relatable."

"Makes sense."

"It did, until the day that Katherine Smith was fully born. Which was also the afternoon after this party."

"Part of me is scared to hear it. The other part of me is hoping you kicked him in the dick."

"You're right on both accounts. I tried to confront him at the office after the party settled down. Maybe not confront, but ask him why he seemingly forgot about me. He wasn't in his office, and no one had seen him. I would've asked the assistant that served the group of mid-level publicists, but she wasn't at her desk either."

"Oh fuck."

"Oh fuck is right." Kat grips on to my arms tighter. "I eventually found them in a stairwell. Let's just say they were using the rails for balance."

"I'm so sorry," I say. "No one should have to catch someone like that."

"It sent me into a rage," she says. "It was my final straw. Once he got his pants up, and the assistant quit acting like she was shocked that I existed, we had it out, in the middle of the office. It was like I had an out-of-body experience and just started screaming. For how he used me. How he was cheating on me. How three days prior he took my lunch that I was looking forward to eating."

"The bastard," I say. "I promise I'll never take your food."

She laughs at my joke. "I don't know who I was at the moment, but I was absolutely causing a scene. I had to get dragged into my boss's office to calm down."

"What happened next?"

"I was suspended for a week and demoted to basically an assistant, with no roles in any accounts. Jeff and what's-her-face got a warning."

"Oh, that would piss me off more than them doing what they did."

"It did. But the boiling point was when I went to his apartment that night to grab my things. I took Logan with me, not wanting to be by myself. Of course, she was there, looking smug as hell, like she won some sort of prize. I asked to talk to him about what happened, not because I'd take him back but...I don't know...I wanted some sort of closure."

"That's understandable. What did he say?"

"That I was getting mad over nothing. That I overestimated how much I helped with his presentation. That I was delusional in thinking that I should get any credit when all I did was type a few slides for him. Oh, and that we weren't that serious, and he doesn't know why I acted how I did. For reference, we were together for a year."

"Mother*fucker*," I growl out. "I fucking hate this guy."

"Join the club. We have matching hats," Kat jokes as she turns around in my arms. "That was the day I realized mixing business and pleasure was the worst idea in the world. That getting your heart broken is one thing, but also someone using you in the work space, copying ideas, all-out using me? Honestly that was harder to get over."

"That's when Katherine was born?"

She nods. "It was a reminder of who I was in that space. Not that I was tempted again, but it was a good insurance policy. Tight buns. Light makeup. Strictly business. That was my persona until Logan told me one day that he wanted to hire me on full-time at GameTech. That I could leave the world where I had to see Jeff every day and get stares from coworkers whom I thought were my friends. The rest is history."

"Except the rule."

"Except the rule." She finally looks up at me, her eyes a little sad, but I see hope in them as well. "I'm scared, Grayson. I know you aren't Jeff. I know that in my bones. But putting myself out there like this when I said I never would again…that's a scary place to be."

"I get that," I say, taking each of her hands in mine and bringing them to my lips. "I know words can be empty sometimes. So me telling you that I'd never use you in that way, or put you in that position, or cheat on you, can only go so far. But please know, I hate liars. And cheaters. I don't even like using cheat codes in video games."

This makes her laugh. "Make sure to tell that to Logan. He appreciates a video game purist."

"I will. I can't wait to meet him." I bring our joined hands between us, laying them over my heart. "Just know that I think you're amazing. Smart. The way you talk to clients…I get now why you beat me. You're fucking brilliant, Katherine Smith. And I'd never want to dull that shine or steal it from you. I'd just be the lucky bastard who gets to be along for the ride."

I watch as a single tear flows down her cheek. I take my thumb and brush it away, making sure to keep my hand exactly where it is.

"Grayson?"

"Yeah Vixen?"

I watch as she gives me a pleading look. "I'm ready."

"For what?"

She puts her free hand over the one that's resting on her cheek. "For you to kiss me."

Five little words. I feel like I've been waiting forever to hear them. It's why I don't wait another second to grant her wish.

Her lips are a little tentative as we meet, but that only lasts for a second until we sink into each other. My hand wraps around the small of her back, bringing her into me as her hands cup my face. It's only been a few days since we've done this, yet it's felt like years. I've missed this. Missed her. The taste of her lips. The way her tongue is always searching for more. How her body melts into me.

Her saying that she was ready for this was a huge step for her. But I know the feeling. Because so am I. I'm ready for it all.

We pull away, just enough to catch our breath, but neither of us move from where we're standing.

"We're doing this, aren't we?"

I nod and tap our foreheads together like I have so many times this weekend. "I'm in if you are."

She lets go of my hands, looping them around my neck to bring me closer. "All in."

17

grayson

I can't believe how much can change in such a short amount of time.

And I'm not just talking about how in a matter of days I went from meeting a woman, falling for her instantly, pretending that I haven't fallen for her when I found out who she was, then falling for her all over again.

No, what's hitting me right now are the little things in that chaos. Like how when we first met, and even when we reconnected here just the other day, our kisses were frantic. It's like we knew we were chasing a hypothetical clock.

But as we ride the elevator up to our room, there's no urgency. There's no one with us, so we could be horny teenagers if we wanted. Continue what we started a few minutes ago. But we don't. Instead I just have her in my arms, holding her tight against me, but nothing that's over the line of PG-rated. We hold hands as we walk to our room. Neither of us are trying to distract each other as I insert the key card to open the door.

Nothing hurried. No ticking time clock.

Just us. And the first night of what I hope are many, many more to come.

"Why again did we stand in the snow for the last hour?" Kat jokes as she steps out of her heels and hands me my jacket.

As soon as both feet are back on the ground, I take her hand and pull her toward me. "So I could do this."

My hand is on the back of her neck, kissing her how I want. Just because this isn't hurried doesn't mean it's not deep. I want to convey how much I want this—how much I heard her earlier —that she's safe with me. That I'd never hurt her. That I want to prove to her how good we can be together.

Kat melts into my hold, her hands gripping onto my shirt to hold her up as our kiss continues to intensify. I could keep us right here and not ruin this perfect moment. But I have a feeling this night is going to be filled with a thousand perfect moments, and those can only happen on the bed.

Well, maybe eight-hundred and fifty of them. Those other hundred and fifty? Those we can get creative with.

As much as it hurts me to do so, I pull away from our kiss, but that's because as much as I've loved looking at her in this Santa outfit—and even though I said I wanted to fuck her while she was wearing it—I want it in a pool at the foot of this bed even more.

I let my hands trail down her arms, tracing each and every inch of her beautiful body down her sides, all the way to the dip of her hips and around the curve of her ass. When my fingers find the edge of the skirt, I gather the dark green fabric in my hands, bringing it up slowly so I can take in every moment.

Her arms slowly raise over her head as the fabric hits her midsection. My eyes go wide once I get a glimpse of the lingerie covering her body.

"Fuck...Kat...you're..."

What even are words?

She's a vision in a black lace, one-piece bodysuit clinging to the curves of her porcelain skin. I can't stop staring. I don't know if it's because the two other times I've seen her like this, it's been a beige set. Don't get me wrong, she's looked like a vision in those as well, but this? This is a garment made for sin...and Kat.

"This is me," she whispers as her arms come down. "The real me."

I reach for her and pull her in, my hands on each ass cheek. "And you're fucking perfect."

My lips are back on hers, hungrily kissing her as we walk back toward the bed. I know I said tonight was about not rushing. That there was no need to. That's not a lie. But seeing her like this—tits spilling over the cups of my favorite piece of clothing ever made—I'm gone. I'm under her spell. She's in my blood.

Right now and forever.

Kat's hands are trying to unbutton my shirt as we fall back into the bed. She has half of them undone before I take over, rising to my knees to finish the job.

"I like this show," she says, raising her arms over her head, posing like a fucking wet dream underneath me.

I grin at her as I unfasten my belt and rip it off of my waist. "Then you're going to love this."

I slide off the bed, but only for the time that I need to strip from my pants and boxer briefs. I remember to grab a condom from my wallet, putting it between my teeth to rip the pack open, sheathing myself as I watch her hand tracing around the edges of the lace.

"Pull it down. I want to see them," I say, stroking my cock as I watch her before me. "Show me how you touch yourself."

She doesn't hesitate, not even for a moment. I watch in awe as she slowly takes one out, then the other. Her eyes are glued to mine as she takes a finger and places it in her mouth, only to let it pop out before she swirls it around her perfect pink nipple.

"Fuck Kat," I groan, starting to stroke myself harder. "Pinch them. Just enough."

Her eyes close as she follows my command, and I can tell the instant she feels the mix of slight pain but so much pleasure. Her pelvis lifts off the bed, as if she's begging her own body to give her more. While I'd love to keep watching her, I'm aching to touch her. To taste her.

Which is exactly what I'm going to do.

"Come here," I say, walking back toward the bed and taking both of her legs in my hands, dragging her closer. "I need to taste you."

I pull the lace to the side, diving in like a man starved. Fuck, I missed this. I realize it's been less than a week since I had her last, but it feels like ages. Probably because the woman has been a walking temptation since the second I saw her in the lobby. And the agony of being so near her the last two nights and not being able to touch her damn near killed me.

Well, until she rolled onto me last night. But I'm going to keep that a secret until she brings it up.

Her hands are gripping onto my hair while also pushing me in for more. I'm sucking on her clit, trying to have my mouth take up as much of her as possible. There's not a drop I'm leaving behind. I could stay here all night—her scent is that intoxicating—but I want something more than that.

I want her.

All of her.

"There's no going back," I say as I move my way up the bed, my fingers now working her. "You ready, Vixen?"

She nods as she wraps her hands behind my neck. "More than ready."

She pulls me in, a kiss so deep that I feel it in every bone in my body. I adjust myself so I can pull her leg up, wrapping it around my hip as I line my cock to her center. She's still wearing the lace, so I make sure it's out of my way. Yes, I could have her take it off, but she looks too fucking good.

I slide in easily, and between how tight she's squeezing me, and the moan that leaves her mouth when I enter her, it's enough to make me come right then and there.

I won't. But I could.

No, I have too much that I want to do, too many ways I want to make her scream. Some of the noises she made that first night are engrained into my memory. But part of me wonders if I made them up. Did it really happen? Did the excitement of that first night together make me conjure some sort of Mandela Effect?

God, I hope not.

"Fucking hell Grayson!" she screams as I start thrusting into her. Her hands are gripped around my biceps, likely leaving marks.

"You're taking me so fucking good," I say, trying my best to go even deeper. "That's it. Every inch, Vixen. Take every single inch."

Her body relaxes into my words, arching slightly to give me a better angle as I continue working her. The tilt of her body presses her tits closer to my face, almost begging me to take one in my mouth. Ha. As if she would ever need to beg me for that.

Her hands move to my back as I dive into her chest, sucking one hard peak while massaging the other. I can't get enough of her. Her body. Every sound she makes. Every involuntary movement she makes. I want to learn them all. I want to memorize each and every one. I want to see Kat come apart in my arms. I want to send Katherine into a tizzy when I rip off that sensible pantsuit she wears and make her bun explode and leave her hair scattered around her shoulders.

I want them all. And I want it with her.

Her legs fall down from my side, and her hands go around my back, as she asks me with her body to turn her over. Again, she'll never have to ask twice. Especially if that means Kat riding me, taking what she wants.

My eyes stay focused on her as she slowly pulls away from me. I expect her to straddle me, and honestly, I can't wait to watch her ride me. Except I watch as she turns around.

"What are you doing, Vixen?"

She looks back over her shoulder, giving me a smile that

screams her nickname. "You told me you wanted me to take every inch, however I wanted. Right?"

"Right."

"Well, that's what I'm doing. You ready?"

I pull her back slightly by her hair, sitting up to put my lips by her ear. "Fuck me like you mean it."

"Be careful what you ask for, Ross."

I kiss her neck. "Do your worst."

This is one position we did not try our first night. Not that I didn't want to, but to me, reverse cowgirl is a position that the woman has to initiate. They're choosing to let their ass bounce on your cock. They're in complete control. And right now, that's exactly what Kat is.

Her hands are gripping my thighs, moving up and down on me just like she promised. My fingers run across the small amount of black lace that wraps around her back, loving the coarse texture against the smoothness of her skin.

I'm getting lost in the feel of her, my eyes shutting as I concentrate on every sensation, when I feel her nails starting to dig into me.

"Grays..." she trails off, but her movements keep going. "I need—"

She doesn't finish her sentence, but somehow, I know what she needs. I put my hands on her hips, guiding her as she circles her hips down into me.

"You did so good," I say, gently lifting her off of me. "Now let me finish."

She nearly falls off of me onto all fours—which might be one of the best views I've ever had in my thirty-four years on this planet. I take her hair in my hand, wrapping the jet-black locks around my fingers as I lean down onto her back, leaving a trail of kisses on her exposed skin as I line myself back up.

The second I'm inside her, our moans coincide, and I'm pretty sure everyone in our hall heard them. The neighbors definitely have to hear the headboard banging against the wall as I drive into her. I don't care. Let them hear. Let them call security. There isn't a single force on this planet right now that could stop me from making this woman come all over my cock.

"Fuck!" she screams out, just as I feel her pussy starting to tighten even more around me.

"That's right, Vixen…come on my cock. You said do your worst. Now do it. And make sure to scream my name when you come."

She turns her head just enough so I can see her brown eyes and flushed cheeks. I don't blink. I squeeze her hips even tighter as I slam into her from behind. And then I send her over the edge with one well-placed smack on the ass.

"Grayson! Fuck! Grayson!"

My name has never sounded better than coming from her lips as she comes apart in front of me.

She drops to her elbows, unable to hold herself up as she continues to unravel. I do my best to help her back up, but seeing her body give out in front of me only makes my release come faster, and before I know it, I'm on top of her, spilling into the condom and fighting for breath.

Neither of us say anything. We don't have to. What we just shared was…there are no words.

Because this is it. What I felt for her on that first night wasn't a flash in a pan. It wasn't one spontaneous night that I romanticized in my head. This was everything.

Just like her.

18
grayson

WHOEVER IS CALLING MY PHONE RIGHT NOW CAN GO STRAIGHT TO hell.

I mean, how dare they call me at—I peek open an eye to see exactly what time it is—8:58 in the morning. Sure, it's not the crack of dawn, but when I have a sleeping, naked, Kat on my chest, under blankets so warm that I never want to leave, anyone calling me at this hour is getting an automatic "fuck you" greeting. I don't care that it's Christmas Eve.

I reach over to grab my phone, ready to silence it, when I see that it's none other than my father calling.

Lovely.

"Good morning, Dad," I groan, trying to wiggle my way from underneath Kat as to not wake her up. "Merry Christmas Eve."

"Where the hell are you?"

Well, that was just a warm greeting.

"I'm in Tennessee. I told you and Mom I was stuck."

"Still?"

So this is how my morning is going to start. Yay.

"Yes, Father. That's what 'snowed in' means," I say as I step into the bathroom and shut the door behind me.

"Well, don't they have snowplows? What kind of state are you living in?"

I pinch the bridge of my nose. I thought not being with my family today would mean I could avoid the annual Christmas migraine. "Dad, as I said to you and Mom when I texted a few days ago, unfortunately, I'm stuck here. Tennessee isn't prepared to handle this kind of snow. It's been going for three days now nonstop. It's not like in Connecticut where everybody and their brother owns a snowplow. The roads and the airports are shut down."

"Well, is it ending anytime soon?"

I love how he thinks I'm suddenly a meteorologist. Though even if I was, I still wouldn't be a coveted lawyer.

"The earliest I'm getting out of here is likely tomorrow night."

"Well, Christmas will be over by then."

Does he not think I don't own a calendar or know how time works? "Yes, Dad. I understand that that's what it means. I'm sorry I'll miss the festivities. Plus, who knows how badly backed up the flights will be. It's probably best that I just stay home this year. I'll try to get there in a few months to see everyone."

"Oh no, you still need to come home," he says in a tone that leaves no room for a negotiation.

"Why are you so hell-bent on this?" I ask. "I'm going to miss tonight and all day tomorrow. The earliest I'd make it back is tomorrow night, but the airports are going to be a madhouse. So for all I know I'll be coming in after midnight. Is me coming home right now really that big of a deal?"

"Ugh!" I feel him rolls his eyes. "You're going to miss it."

"Christmas?" I ask. "I mean, is Santa Claus himself coming? I feel like he knows the weather and will understand why I can't make it."

"Why are you being a smartass about this?" he huffs. "You're going to miss the big announcement."

"What announcement?"

"We were going to wait until the whole family was together

—all of the uncles, aunts, and cousins—and we thought Christmas dinner would be the best place."

"Well, don't keep me waiting Dad. I'm on the edge of my seat."

"Your sister is getting married."

That's the announcement? I mean, good for her. But she's dated the same guy since freshman year of college. If they broke up, that would be bigger news.

"Thanks for letting me know. I'll call her and congratulate her."

"But that's not the exciting news. Her fiancé is leaving his firm in Boston. The two are going to be taking over Ross and Family next year when I retire."

Of course my father would prioritize the law firm over an engagement.

"Good for them."

"That's it?"

Really? He's surprised by my reaction? "What do you want me to say, Dad?"

"I want to hear some enthusiasm in your voice. You should be proud of your sister and how hard she's worked."

"Just like she's proud of me?" I ask.

"You know it's not the same."

"That's the one thing in this life I do know."

"It doesn't have to be this way," he says. And here it comes: the yearly guilt treatment of me not being a part of the firm. It's like getting socks in my stocking, you can count on it every Christmas. "How does it feel knowing that you're the only family member that's not carrying on the tradition?"

"Actually, it feels pretty good," I say. "I'm happy. I have a job I'm good at. I like the city I live in. And I just started seeing someone. Everything's coming up Grayson."

As if on cue, Kat opens the bathroom door. I bite my bottom lip as I stare at her wearing my button-down from last night.

"You're seeing someone? So you're actually going to, what,

stay in Nashville?" He says it like I've decided to live in a third-world country with no indoor plumbing.

"Yeah, Dad. For the foreseeable future, I am," I say, signaling for Kat to come sit on my lap. "Her name is Kat. Short for Katherine. Not like a cat. That was my first mistake too."

She smiles as she loops her hands around my neck. "Dad, I don't want to be a lawyer. I don't want to move back to Connecticut so you and the uncles can live out this weird fantasy of everyone in the bloodline working at the law firm. I'm happy with my life. My career. My choices. I am successful by anyone's definition. And if you're not okay with all that, then maybe I won't see you for Christmas next year either."

"You wouldn't. What would I tell your mother?"

"Easy. Tell her that her son is going to spend time with people who make him happy and accept his choices. If she, or you, don't understand that, then we have nothing more to talk about."

This makes him go silent. And you know what, this conversation is over.

"Dad, I'm sorry that I'm missing the big announcement, and you know, the actual holiday. We'll talk soon."

He clears his throat before speaking. "Yes, son. Merry Christmas."

We both hang up, and I let out the biggest, and most relieved, breath I've had in a long time.

"Everything okay? It didn't sound like a pleasant conversation."

"It wasn't," I say. "But at the same time, I feel better than I have in ages."

"Wanna talk about it?" she asks.

"Not in the least," I say, pulling her in tighter.

"Well, what do you want to do? Reclaim our table from yesterday and open the laptops? Sit here all day and find twenty-four hours of Christmas movies?"

I shake my head. "No work. Starting right now, we're both on vacation."

This makes her smile. "Vacation, huh? What do you have in mind?"

I pretend to think for a second, even though I already have something in mind. "I'm thinking something outside-y."

She raises an eyebrow. "Not outdoorsy, right?"

I kiss her nose. "Absolutely not."

———

"This feels pretty fucking outdoorsy."

I laugh as Kat scrunches her nose and mumbles random swear words as we walk up the sledding hill on the grounds of the Timberline.

"It's not that outdoorsy," I defend.

She stops and points to the sled we're carrying. "I'm walking up a hill. In snow. With boots on. And not cute ones. I'm helping carry a sled. That I'm going to use to slide down a hill in the cold with snow blowing in my face. And then I have to climb back up the hill again. If that's not outdoorsy, I don't know what is."

She has a point, but I need to hold my ground. "Okay, it's in the middle. But it's going to be fun. Plus, it could be worse."

"How?"

We stop at the top of the hill, and I lean in toward her. "We could be going on a hike."

"You wouldn't dare."

"Never." I peck a kiss to her lips before arranging the sled on the top of the hill. When I stand back up, I see her looking around, a bit confused.

"Everything okay?" I ask.

"Yeah. Just wondering how this goes."

I give her a confused stare. "How what goes?"

"How does this work?" Kat points to the sled. "Like, how do

we move? How does it go? Is there an engine I missed? I don't understand the mechanics."

"Kat, have you never gone sledding before?"

"This is actually my first snow."

That takes me back. "Your first snow?"

She nods, suddenly a little shy. "You have to remember, I'm a born and raised California kid, and not in the area where they do get some snow each year. This is my second Christmas in Tennessee, but the only snow we got last year was when I happened to be away for work. So yeah, all of this is a first for me."

Wow…I never even thought of that. And now I'm even more glad that I stretched the limits of her outdoorsy and outside-y rule.

When you're in your thirties, there are less and less firsts to be had. Sure, marriage and kids are there. Some big life experiences. But these littles ones? Ones that normally wouldn't be a big deal, but when you get to watch the person you're falling for more and more experience them? Those are the ones you're going to treasure.

And it being on Christmas Eve? There's something poetic about that.

"Well then…" I pull her into me, giving her a quick, and family friendly, kiss. "Let me show you how it's done."

I make sure the sled is situated perfectly on the hill—flat enough that we can get in it, but not so far away we can't catch the slope.

"Get in, toward the front," I instruct, which she does. I move it up a little closer before I situate myself. "Now come here."

I spread my legs, bringing her back tight into my hold. She turns her head just as I wrap my arms around her.

"If you wanted me to cuddle you like this, we could've stayed in the room and done warm, inside-y things."

I chuckle. "We'll have plenty of time to do that later. Now, when I give the go, we're both going to push off with our hands.

A few shoves and we should be at the hill and then gravity takes us the rest of the way."

"Just for clarification, when I said outside-y things, I meant being pulled in a sleigh drinking hot chocolate."

"I'll remember that for next time. Three…two…one…push!"

Despite her objections, Kat reaches her gloved hands into the snow and we start inching our way to the drop of the hill. Luckily, the hill is pretty steep, so we only need a little bit of momentum before we catch the incline.

"Here we go!"

The word isn't out of my mouth before we start shrieking in excitement. My hands are back around Kat, making sure she's secure as our speed kicks up.

"My God!" she yells, laughter and happiness radiating from her voice. She even gives a good "Woohoo!", which I never thought I would hear out of her smart and sometimes sarcastic mouth. But in this moment, it's the most beautiful noise in the world.

The bottom of the hill is coming sooner rather than later, but I didn't realize that it's coming abruptly. I do my best to try to shift our body weight to help with the braking, but it doesn't work, and before I know it, we're hitting the flat and tumbling from the sled.

We're both laughing as we roll in the snow, the sled slipping out from underneath us once we hit the ground. Every part of me is covered in snow except my face. I'm still holding onto Kat, who's now on her back, and she's covered in the fresh, white powder.

"Are you okay?" I ask, even though the smile on her face and the red in her cheeks tells me everything is fine.

"I'm surprisingly good." She tilts her head down, finding my lips in a kiss that's innocent enough, but if we were alone, and not in the cold, could turn very inappropriate, very quick. "Maybe outdoorsy things aren't so bad."

"Really?" I can't contain my excitement, and I'm already

brainstorming five different trips we could take. "Maybe a ski trip in the future?"

"Maybe. The wardrobe's really cute."

I smile as I push a tendril of her hair back behind her ear and inside the wool beanie. "It also has fireplaces and warm lounges and some of the best drinks you'll ever have."

"Now you're talking. Make me one promise though."

"Anything."

"Can we please go inside? I'm fucking freezing."

I laugh and kiss her one more time. "Gladly."

———

You'd think I'd be buried inside Kat the way I just moaned. Except I'm not. No, the only other thing in this hotel room that could make me let out a sound like that is the hot water coming out of this shower head.

It's perfect, and the perfect end to a perfect afternoon.

After we grabbed lunch—which consisted of a whole lot of soup—the only thing either of us wanted to do was take a nap before getting ready for the Christmas Eve dinner the Timberline is hosting tonight. I slept for about forty-five minutes, and when I woke up, all I heard were Kat's adorable snores as she was curled up under the blankets and into me. Not wanting to disturb her, I decided to jump in the shower and let her sleep a little longer.

I crack my neck, twisting it back and forth, as the hot water runs down my face and body. Normally when I do this, I'm working out the kinks from the stress of work—or I just talked to my family. But right now, I'm more relaxed than I've been in a very long time.

Yes, a lot of that has to do with the woman sleeping in the next room. But a lot of it has to do with the fact that for the first time in my life, I'm spending Christmas Eve the way I want to. I'm not arguing with my father. I'm not trying to appease my mother. I'm not trying to act interested in cases my siblings are talking about or wondering when, if ever, they're going to ask me about anything that has to do with my life or my career.

Instead, I had an amazing day with a beautiful woman. It was nothing but smiles and laughter and conversation that never seemed to end. Tonight is going to be a nice dinner followed by an even better night in our room. It's not going to be me counting down the hours until my flight home to Connecticut. The opposite. If I could freeze time right now, I would. Because this is, without a doubt, the best Christmas I've ever had.

I close my eyes as I start to wash my face when I feel a burst of cold air hit my back.

"Want some company?"

I turn around to the best sight I have ever, and likely, will ever see. A naked Kat, walking toward me, her hair down and resting on her shoulders, her cheeks pink from slight windburn.

Sheer and utter perfection.

"Always. Come here, Vixen."

I pull her into me, letting the water from the shower head rain down on us. "Did I wake you?

"No. But when I heard the water, I couldn't resist."

"I'm glad." I turn her around, her back to my front as I stand directly under the spray. "Let's warm you up."

I let my hands run over her smooth skin, kissing down her neck as the water cascades down. Her hands reach up and back around my neck, giving me all the access I could ever want to touch every inch of her perfect body.

"I'm going to miss this," she says.

"Miss what?"

"Hotel showers with you." She turns around, her hands staying wrapped around my neck. "I've become quite accustomed to them."

"Well, then, let's make this one count."

I reach over to the ledge and grab her shampoo, squeezing some into my hands, the relaxing smell hitting me immediately.

"Is this…eucalyptus?"

I gather her hair in my hands, beginning to work in the suds.

"Tea tree," she says. "Isn't the smell amazing?"

"It is," I say, but it's not just the smell of the shampoo. It's this. All of this. For the first time in my life, I feel like everything is going the way I want. I have a woman I'm crazy about. Even though senior account executive might not be in the near future, I feel like I'm out of the rut I was in with my job. And standing up to my parents and putting some distance between myself and them? I've felt twenty pounds lighter since I hung up that phone today.

Yes, it's like I got everything I wanted for Christmas, and none of it is what I asked for.

"God, that feels so good." Her words come out in a moan. "When we're back in Nashville and not in a hotel, can you still do this?"

"The day I turn down a shower with you is the day I forget how to breathe."

I turn her around, continuing to massage her head as I rinse out the soap, taking in every second of beauty and relaxation on Kat's face. When it's all rinsed out, I can't help myself from kissing her. She's an absolute vision right now. Our lips are hungry for each other, and before long, I feel her hands running down my chest, heading to where I want her to touch me more than I want anything right now.

"Already hard for me?" she asks as she wraps both hands around me.

"For you? Always."

Not wanting to be left out of the fun, I take both of her tits in each of my hands, rubbing them together as the water falls off of them. Our eyes are locked. The heat passing through them is palpable. It's more than just want. It's more than giving each other the release we know the other can provide.

This is true connection. Something that you don't find every day. Something you find randomly, on a Thursday night, with a woman wearing an ugly Christmas sweater.

Something you find once—if you're lucky—in this lifetime.

"Turn around," I say, but not before sucking on her nipple quickly and letting go with a pop. Except when I do, I realize that we're in the shower, and since I didn't plan on her coming in with me, I didn't bring in a condom. "Fuck, "I don't have a—"

She puts a finger to my lips. "I'm clean. I have an IUD. And I trust you."

The last admission hits me square in the chest. "I promise, I am too. And I've never not used one."

I watch in awe as Kat does what I ask, turning herself around, holding onto the wall of the shower, bending over to the perfect angle for me to slide right into her. "Then take me, Grayson. Just us."

I'm a bull seeing red. Between her delicious ass waiting for me, her eyes looking at me over her shoulder, begging me to take her, I couldn't hold back if I wanted to.

"Just us," I grit out, stroking myself one last time before I line myself up at her, sliding in with so much ease that the sound that I let out isn't human.

"Holy fuck, Kat," I say, quickly becoming overwhelmed at the feel of her against my bare cock. "You feel so fucking good."

"You always do," she says, bending over a little more for me. "Yes, right there."

My hands are gripping her waist as I drive into her—the screams she's making are enough to send me over the edge, but I won't. I force back my orgasm, not ready for this scene to end quite yet. But what I do want to happen is watch from this angle as Kat comes apart, and I know just what will send her there.

"Grayson! Ah!"

The scream is loud enough to travel through our room and down the hallway as I rub on her clit, already having memorized exactly how she likes to be touched there and what button to push to send her into orbit.

"Fuck, fuck!" she yells as she slams back into me just as hard as I'm driving into her. "Ah!"

The scream is deafening, and frankly, if that's the last sound I ever hear, I'll die a happy man. Kat is shaking from the orgasm, and my arms wrap around her to hold her still. In watching her completely come apart, I don't realize until it's too late that I'm following behind her, my balls tightening before I feel my orgasm explode inside of me.

My hands are digging into her hips, desperate to hold onto her as I spill myself inside her. Thank God there's a shower seat in here, which is what Kat's using now to hold herself up, both of us about ready to collapse.

"What are you doing to me?" she asks with stuttering breaths as I slowly pull myself of her, my chest collapsing on her back.

"I was going to ask you the same thing."

I don't know what this is—whether it's love or lust or like, or a combination of those.

But I know it's special. Rare. That if I don't hold onto this, I might not ever find something like this again.

And it's why I have no plans on letting go.

guide to christmas (and love) rule #89

Be careful what you wish for. Even at Christmas.

19
kat

I wake up to Grayson's sweet words and his lips on my forehead as I cuddle into him tighter. "Merry Christmas to you too."

It's been a long time since I've woken up in the arms of the same man numerous, and consecutive, days in a row. And that man was Jeff—also known as the distant sleeper. He never argued about what side of the bed I wanted; he just wanted to make sure there was space between us. The pillow fort Grayson built the first night? That actually would've been Jeff's dream.

Then there's Grayson, who when I made a joke last night before we finally went to bed about making the wall again, had the exact words of "fuck the pillow fort" before pulling me into his hold. Once last night I rolled away, as my shoulder was starting to hurt, and before I knew it, I was right back in his arms —new position, but same grasp.

It's becoming addicting. A thought that should scare me, but weirdly doesn't. What's going to happen tonight when we don't sleep next to each other? The snow stopped last night, so I know today's our final day at the Timberline. Logan has the jet ready to take me to St. Lucia, but I'm not sure if Grayson is going back to Nashville or headed to his parents in Connecticut. Would he want to come to the beach with me? Could he? Is it weird if I ask? Am I needy if I do? Am I a bitch if I don't? What are the rules? Why is there not some guide to love that gives women the road map of how to navigate a relationship?

Oh…I should write one…

"What kind of Christmas Day do you have?"

His question pulls me from my random thoughts of getting into the publishing game. "What kind of day?"

"Yeah. What's your Christmas routine? I find it fascinating how everyone grows up thinking their way of Christmas is the only way, only to find out that everyone does things slightly different."

"I don't know about that, I feel like my way is pretty common." I say as I roll over, wanting to look at him in the lazy morning light. "After my dad left, Mom and I made it a point each Christmas to never get out of our pajamas. It wasn't an f-you to him, just something we started doing together to make a new tradition. Breakfast consisted of cookies, cinnamon rolls, and absolutely nothing healthy. We'd open presents—stockings first, because we're not psychopaths—and then after, we just laid around all day watching whatever we felt like putting on, and then ordered Chinese food for dinner."

That makes Grayson laugh. "Really? Pajamas all day and Chinese for dinner? I heard that they're one of the few restaurants open on Christmas, but I never met anyone who actually got it on Christmas."

"It was our favorite," I say. "Also, Mom was never a big cooker. She always argued why should she have to do something that she doesn't like on a holiday?

"As someone who just implemented that rule in his life, I respect her outlook."

"It made the day fun. Low stress. A true day of spending time together and just unwinding."

"Also known as the exact opposite of my family growing up."

"Let me guess, your family has an agenda and a timed itinerary?"

"It's an unofficial one, but it exists," he says.

"Shit. I was joking."

"Oh, there's no joking about the strict schedule of a Ross Christmas. And it doesn't matter how big the family is, how many grandchildren are added to the mix, the day is set in stone and cannot be moved."

"We wake up sharply at eight-thirty in the morning. Which is fine as adults, but setting an alarm as a child, knowing that when it went off you could leave your room was…something. But that's because no one is allowed to go into the family room until my mother gives the go-ahead. You know, to make sure everything is perfect for the family picture."

"Nothing like a forced family photo to show how happy everyone is."

"Exactly," she says with a laugh. "Wait. If you're taking a perfect family photo, does that mean you…dress up?"

He laughs. "Oh yes. Tie and all. How else are we supposed to show up to the formal breakfast?"

Kat's eyes about pop out of her head. "Back the fuck up. You're telling me that as a child, knowing that Santa came last night and there were presents about, that you had to get fully dressed in uncomfortable clothes and eat a multi-course breakfast before you could open presents?"

"And no one could leave until everyone was done. Which was the worst when my brother was going through a phase where he refused to eat eggs. In all my years, I don't think a single present has been opened before ten."

"Wow," Kat says in disbelief. "I know you and I are just getting started, but can I petition that we spend Christmas with my mother—or anywhere but Connecticut?"

He laughs. "You haven't heard the worst of it. That formal breakfast is followed by presents, which takes hours because my grandmother is insistent we all open one at a time, and we also can't have our phones out during the process. Oh and did I mention that it's my entire family? Aunts, uncles, cousins, and their partners and kids? It takes forever. By the time we're done and everyone is miserable, it's time for lunch, which is a respectable spread of sandwiches and appetizers, before the family photo, and then dinner to be served promptly at six p.m."

"Where do the cookies fit in?" Kat asks. "Cookies are an important part of Christmas, and the fact that you haven't mentioned them yet worries me."

He shakes his head, and my jaw drops.

"Are you telling me that you are a cookie-less family?"

"The only ones we ever saw were the ones we left for Santa."

"That's... I don't even know what to say. It's just wrong."

"That's a Ross Christmas for you."

"Well that's not how you're spending this year," I say, sitting up off the bed. "Put your pajamas on."

He raises an eyebrow. "You want me to get out of bed to put on my sleeping clothes?"

"Exactly." I move closer so I can straddle him, figuring that my boobs in his face will make him agree with my idea. "We're going to go downstairs and eat breakfast. If you order one egg, you're doing this wrong. Today is about carbs and sugar. And I have on good authority that they are serving cinnamon rolls, waffles, and pancakes with nothing healthy on the side."

"And we're doing this in our pajamas?"

"Exactly. And then when we're done, we're going to go into the kitchen and steal every last Christmas cookie there is."

"Is there any protein in today's diet?"

"Not a lick. Because when we get back to the room, our day is going to consist of Christmas movies, cookies, naps, and sex."

Grayson's smile can't be contained. "A day of nothing but cookies and sex?"

"And naps."

"Of course."

"How does that sound for our first Christmas together?"

His smile is as bright as any Christmas tree lights. "Sounds like the best Christmas I've ever had."

————

"How am I stuffed when all I had was empty calories and powdered sugar?"

I gently dab my mouth after swallowing my last bite of banana foster french toast. "It was those eggs that I gave in and let you eat. The protein messed up the balance."

"I needed my strength," he says with a laugh before leaning in close. "I do remember that sex was a part of the agenda today. You don't want me passing out, do you?"

"We can't have that," I say, my body heating just thinking about Christmas sex. Which I have to assume ranks at the top of all days to have sex. "If you want one more, you can have it."

He kisses my hand before sitting back. "No, I can't eat another bite. Though I am ready for my afternoon of fun that also included cookies and naps."

"Say no more." I put down my napkin before standing up. "I'm going to go break into the kitchen. Are you coming with me for the Christmas heist?"

He shakes his head. "I'm going to wait for our server to come back. Make sure he's taken care of. And the others who are working today."

You can tell a lot about a man on how he treats the wait staff. And if he's doing what I think he's about to do, this man just earned a long, afternoon blowjob.

"That's really nice of you," I lean down and kiss him. "Chip in extra for me too, okay?"

He nods. "You got it. Meet you at the elevator?"

"Sounds good."

I give him one more kiss before I start making my way to the kitchen, hoping there's a worker who I've met over the last few days who can sneak me back for some treats. I have no clue if there are actually cookies back there, but there have to be a few, right?

"Ho! Ho! Ho! Merry Christmas!"

I smile as I turn to the sound of a voice I don't think I'm going to forget for a very long time. "How am I ever going to start my day without my very own Santa greeting me?"

"Oh I'm sure you'll figure something out," he says. "Merry Christmas, Katherine."

"Merry Christmas, Howard."

We embrace in a hug before Howard hands me a gift bag.

"Howard, you didn't have to do that."

"Oh it's nothing," he says. "Just a little something to make up for the room mix-up, the snow, and having to spend your Christmas here with us."

"It's no problem," I say, looking over to Grayson, who is currently being squeezed by the waiter, whom I'm pretty sure just got the tip of his life. "It turned out to be a pretty good few days."

That makes Howard smile. "I see that. I'm glad the Timberline can be part of your story."

"I'll always remember it," I say. "And maybe it'll be a little more memorable if there happen to be any Christmas cookies laying around?"

He smiles and nods his head toward the kitchen. "Follow me. I'll show you my secret stash."

"You're the best."

Howard leads me back through the kitchen and back into a large pantry. "Let's see…what do I have?"

I was just hoping for a few chocolate chips and maybe some sugar cookies. But what Howard pulls out of the cupboard in a plastic bag is enough to get Grayson and I through New Years.

"Here you go. Want some milk to go with them?"

I shake my head. "Howard, you don't have to give me your entire stockpile."

"You think that's all I have? That was my *tomorrow* bag."

I laugh as I take them from him. "Well, thank you. Grayson and I both appreciate it."

"So where to when you leave this place?"

"St. Lucia," I say. "A few days of sun and a beach. I enjoyed the snow, but I'm a warm-weather girl at heart."

"When are you leaving?"

"Seven o'clock, as long as the roads are clear."

"Oh, tonight?"

"Is that a problem? I thought the roads were set to open."

"They are," he says, suddenly seeming like he's scrambling. "Before you leave, do you have time to meet with Declan and I?"

"Yeah, sure," I stutter out. "Do you want to meet now and get it out of the way?"

He shakes his head. "Oh no. I don't want to ruin the last little bit of time you have here today. Maybe around four, before you head to the airport?"

"That's fine." I say, except that it's not fine because why is he being so cryptic. "Is everything okay?"

He can't hide the smile. "Let's just say, it's very good news."

I should be happy, but a sense of dread comes over me. "Okay. I'll see you then."

Howard leads me out of the kitchen before walking away, and I'm left standing there confused. What would he want to talk to me about besides...

Shit. They're picking me.

I've never been so disappointed to get a client in all my years in PR.

Honestly, in the blissfulness of the past couple days, I almost forgot that's why we were here in the first place. But that has to be what he wants to talk about. I can't imagine they'd ask to talk to me just to let me down easy.

But...shit...Grayson. Did I want to win? Yes. But, I don't want to beat him again. From the little bits I gathered, he had a good presentation. He had good ideas. It feels...don't know, it feels wrong. Is this my feelings for him clouding my reaction? I don't think so, but they don't help.

Does he know yet? Is that why they didn't want to meet now? That would be pretty shitty of Howard to tell me, knowing I'd still see Grayson before I left.

I suck in a breath and walk back through the restaurant toward the elevator. Except Grayson is still at our table, looking at something on his phone.

I stop to look at him, trying to read his face. It's like he can feel my eyes on him, because he looks up, and his face is white, and he just looks…sad.

Fuck. Is this it? I don't want to assume, but there's nothing in his expression right now that gives me any sort of hope.

The realist in me takes center stage. I thought we could mix business and pleasure. I should've known it was a pipe dream. Because seeing his face now? He doesn't have to say anything.

We're over before we even began.

20
grayson

I DIDN'T MEAN TO CHECK MY EMAIL. I JUST HAPPENED TO HAVE MY phone out when I got a message I truly didn't expect to get any day, let alone on Christmas Day.

Grayson,
Merry Christmas and I hope your trip to Connecticut has been going well. I wanted to message you that, since you'll be up there for a few days, maybe swing into New York and do some apartment hunting. There's been a retirement in the New York office, meaning there's a position open for a senior account executive. The job is yours. You earned it.
We'll talk more when we're back after the first of the year. Congratulations again.
Merry Christmas,
Melinda

Holy shit...this...I have to read it three times because never on any bingo card or prediction betting block did I have getting this email today.

Melinda wants to give me the job of my dreams. Sure, I want

it. This is all I've ever wanted since my first day as a junior executive with a box full of things for a cubicle desk and a dream.

But it's in New York.

Closer to my family.

Further away from the life I've built.

Further away from Kat.

My gut reaction is to not take it. Maybe not respond to Melinda today, but soon. I'll just tell her that I'm happy where I am in Nashville, and I'd rather wait for a spot to come open there than move to New York. But I can't let that thought process before I feel Kat's eyes on me. I don't know how, but I feel her presence before I see her. When I look up and we make eye contact, she looks just as worried as I know I probably do. I don't even have a second to try to figure out what she's thinking before she takes off toward the elevator.

"Kat!" I yell, standing up so quick that I knock down the chair. "Kat! Wait!"

I'm in a full-on sprint through the Timberline lobby, and the only reason I catch up to her is because she's waiting on the elevator.

"Hey." I grab her wrist so she'll turn around and look at me, which is the first time that I see the tears pooling in her eyes. "Kat…"

I can't say or do anything else as the elevator arrives. I don't know what she's sad about or if she's just going off of my reaction to the email. I want to explain everything, tell her that I'm not taking the job. But not here, in an elevator, with a family stepping in with us.

"Everything's going to be okay," I whisper as I hold her hand.

She doesn't say anything. Neither of us do until we're back into our room. And even then, Kat's silent as she pulls from my hold, instead heading straight to her luggage.

"Are you leaving earlier than expected?"

She shakes her head. "Just getting ready."

"For what?"

She stops at that question, slowly turning around. "The inevitable."

Okay, I definitely feel like we're reading two different books now. "Can we back up? What's going on in that head of yours?"

She doesn't say anything, instead still continuing to throw her clothes haphazardly into her suitcase. "Kat, talk to me."

My hand on her shoulder is the only thing that stops her whirlwind of motions. But when she turns around, it's the single tear falling down her cheek that breaks me.

"The Timberline. I got it."

Four days ago, those five words would've sent me into a blind rage. I'd be cursing out a woman named Katherine Smith and pouting about another notch in my loss column. Yet all I feel is pure excitement for her.

"That's amazing," I say, bringing her into my arms. "I'm so proud of you."

She shakes her head and pushes out of my hold. "You're proud of me?"

"Of course I am. It was a good presentation, and Declan and Howard seemed to like it. Of course I'm proud of you."

Her eyes are squinting as if she's trying to see something on me that she can't quite make out. "You're not mad?"

"I'm not."

"But they sent you the email."

I check my phone quickly, but I don't see anything. "Not yet, but I'm sure it's coming."

"Then what were you reading on your phone that had you cosplaying as Casper?"

I didn't know how to bring this up, but I guess now's as good of a time as any. "I got an email from my boss."

She wasn't expecting that. "Your boss? On Christmas?"

I nod and sit on the bed, patting the seat next to me, asking her to come sit by me. I hold in a breath until she makes her way toward me.

"Apparently I'm getting an unexpected Christmas gift...in the form of a new title."

"Oh. Wait! Did you—"

I nod. "You're looking at Sterling Strategies' newest senior account executive."

Now it's Kat's turn to be thrilled. "Oh my God, that's amazing!"

She starts to hug me, but quickly realizes I'm not sharing in the enthusiasm.

"Why aren't you excited? This is what you wanted!"

I nod. "It's in New York."

It takes a few seconds for her to process what I just said. But I can tell the second it does.

"Oh."

"Yeah," I say, holding her hand and lacing our fingers together. "Everything I thought I wanted. Merry Christmas to me."

The silence is deafening. I know it's only seconds, but it feels like hours that neither of us even breathe. The tension hasn't been this thick in the room since our first day here. It's amazing how much things can change in such a short amount of time. Because I just got the job offer of my dreams after meeting the girl of my dreams.

And I don't think I can have both. At least not right now.

"I'm turning it down."

"What!" Kat yells, turning toward me. "Did I just hear you right?"

I nod. "Yeah, it's fine. There will be other promotions."

"Like hell it's fine!"

That wasn't the reaction I was expecting. "Kat, it's my decision. I don't want to move to New York."

"Really?" she asks. "You don't want to be a big wig? You don't want that office? You don't want the job and the promotion you've been working toward for years? Think about it, Grayson. Really, truly, sit back and think about this."

"But—"

"No buts," she says. "And don't think about me. Don't think about your family. Just think about you. What is it that you want?"

I want it all, but I know that I can't have it.

Which fucking sucks.

Yes, I want her. I want to know what would come when we get back to Nashville and start really exploring this draw between us. We'd learn to navigate the ropes of our relationship, doing our best to support each other in our careers while also giving each other the space we need to do what we do best. Will we work? I hope we do. But at the end of the day, I've known this woman for a week. Everything I'm wishing for is based on hope and the false sense of reality of living in a bubble with her for the past five days.

Then there's New York. A place I know and have friends. My family would be a train ride away, if I ever decide to visit them again. It's a city I'm familiar with and doing the job that I've wanted since I signed my first tax form at Sterling Strategies.

How can I turn it down? Sure, my gut said to, but that's just it, a gut reaction. When I turn to look at Kat, her eyes are sympathetic, clearly having got to where I'm just arriving a long time ago.

"It was always going to be tough," she says, her voice shaking.

"It shouldn't have to be like this."

She nods, bringing our joined hands to her free one. "We were just getting started. We have no idea where this was going or where it would've ended up, but this is your dream. And if there's anyone who knows what it takes to get there, and how hard you have to work for this, it's me. You have to take it, Grayson."

The silence is back, only this time instead of being tense, I swear I can see both of our brains playing the last week of our lives on repeat.

I remember seeing her at the bar at speed dating. Her smile lit up the room. She was pretending to laugh at whatever joke the guy in front of me told, and I could tell she was being polite. It's why I felt such a sense of pride later when I got a genuine laugh from her.

I'm going to miss that laugh. That smile. How she curls up to me in bed. The snores. Fuck, I'm going to miss those.

I'm going to miss her. But she's right. If I turn this down, I can't assume another one of these chances will come up. And even if it does, how long will that be? There's no guarantees on anything.

I have to take it.

But fuck, I don't want to.

"We had a lot of fun." I say, unable to force back the tears forming in my eyes.

"Maybe the best Christmas I've had in years," she says, her tears matching mine.

"I don't know if I'll ever be able to play trivia again."

That makes her laugh. "Even if you do, you won't win."

"Then what's the point?"

We share a smile as I bring her into my arms. "I'd be a selfish bastard if I asked you to come to New York, right?"

"Not selfish, but I can't," she says. "My life is in Nashville. But you…you're about to have one in New York, and it's going to be amazing."

"I don't want to lose you." I kiss her temple, knowing in my gut that this is probably the last time I'm going to get to hold her in my arms. "There has to be a way."

Kat shakes her head. "We could lie to ourselves and say that we'll try long distance, and it would probably work for a little bit. But we both know how this job goes. It starts with one missed trip here, one crisis there. Next thing we know, we've been reduced to a few emails a week and four canceled trips that we promised we're going to make up to the other."

She's right on every point. I fucking hate it.

"This fucking sucks," I say. "I don't want it to end this way."

"Neither do I. But it just wasn't our time. Or maybe it was."

That takes me back. "How?"

She sits up, but keeps hold of my hand. "I believe that every person comes in your life for a reason. And you…you made me realize that I could be both of me in one. I honestly don't know if I ever would have got there had it not been for you. Thank you for that."

My heart aches with her words, but I know exactly what she means. "And you…you made me look inside myself and push myself to be better. I didn't want to admit it, but I was stuck before you. I know I said it before, but you, Katherine Smith, have made me better."

The tears are pooling again in those brown eyes that I've come to love so much. "You're going to do great things, Grayson Ross."

I tap my forehead to your hers. "But never as good as you."

———

I can't be in this room anymore.

It's been two hours since my talk with Kat and one since she packed up her things and left. We both agreed that spending the day together, waiting for our flights, would lead to only more heartbreak and sadness. She told me I could stay, that she had to meet with Howard and Declan before she could go to the airport to get her flight.

That left me here. Alone. Thinking of every memory that was created here in the past five days.

And I fucking hate it.

My bags are packed. That took me all of four seconds. I checked my email, and like I knew was coming, I saw one in there from Declan and Howard. I didn't bother opening it. I know what it says. And while I'm happy for Kat, I don't need salt in a wound today.

I should head to the airport. Wait for a standby flight to New York. The one I don't want to take. But I don't. Instead I'm going to wallow on this bed—the one I'd planned on laying in all day with Kat in my arms—as I stuff myself with the Christmas cookies she left and watching some Christmas movie where the guy *does* get the girl at Christmas.

Lies. All lies. People don't end up together at Christmas. Maybe I should call one of my family members and sue this channel for spreading false hope and misinformation.

I'm startled when I hear my phone ringing, and even more surprised when I see that it's Melinda calling.

"Hey, boss. Merry Christmas." I move out of the bed, hoping that sitting in an actual chair will make me put on a better front. "Didn't expect to hear from you twice in a day."

"And I expected to hear from you at least once," she says. "I know you're with your family, but I figured that email would at least elicit a response."

Shit. In the craziness of the morning, I never even thought to send back an email even saying thanks. "Sorry, it's been a crazy morning."

"Crazy? You told me last year about your family's Christmas itinerary. How does that mean crazy?"

"Oh…yeah…I never made it to Connecticut."

"What? Where are you?"

"I'm still at the Timberline. We didn't make it out in time and got snowed in."

"Are you serious?" she says. "You've been there the whole time? And wait…who's we?"

Shit. I didn't mean to say that or forget to tell her that I've been here since Saturday. "Remember Katherine Smith?"

"Is that the woman who made you get the villain look in your eye, thinking about how you were going to take her down?"

I laugh. "Yeah, that's her. Turns out the Timberline was talking to her as well."

"Well how about that," Melinda says, amusement in her voice. "I'm not going to ask for details, because I'm still your boss. But is she the reason I didn't get an immediate excited phone call this morning?"

"She is," I say, taking in a deep breath before I put this all out there. "This…don't get me wrong, I'm honored and flattered that you and the partners want to promote me. It's all I've ever wanted. It's just…"

"Now there's something more than work to think about?"

"Exactly," I say. "I'm not turning it down. But…can I have a few days to think about this? For me to sit back and think and for the two of us to talk maybe sometime next week?"

"Absolutely," she says. "I worded that email because I knew the Grayson that left here a few days ago. That's what I get for assuming you didn't go to an inn in the mountains and fall in love over Christmas."

I laugh. "It sounds fictional, doesn't it?"

"It sounds like a love story for the ages."

guide to christmas (and love) rule #133

Don't worry if you don't like what you got for Christmas. That's why returns exist. And apologies.

21
kat

LOGAN

Merry Christmas, Kat.

KAT

Merry Christmas. Already open all the presents?

The little man was up and ready to go at six. We held him off until seven. But it was worth every second.

That's good.

I wanted to let you know that the plane is ready for whenever you want to go. They have the all clear.

Okay. Thanks. I'll make my way over there soon.

Is everything okay?

I HATE THAT MY BEST FRIEND KNOWS ME SO WELL THAT EVEN OVER text message, he can tell that I'm not myself. And because I haven't immediately responded, a phone call is coming in three…two…

"What's the matter?"

I laugh through a threatening tear. I really don't want to cry in public more than I already have. Sure, I'm tucked away in a back corner of the Timberline where I don't think anyone has realized that I'm hanging out, but still, we don't need a breakdown. Not on Christmas.

"Nothing," I lie, closing my eyes to keep in the tears. "Just been a hard morning."

"What happened? Did something happen with Grayson? Did he hurt you? Kat, I swear to God—"

"No, nothing like that," I quickly say. "The only thing that hurt me was life."

I go on to tell Logan about the last few days. How Grayson and I have come together. How we really saw a future with each other when we got back to Nashville. Then, I fast forwarded to today. Me and the Timberline. Grayson and his promotion. The fact that it's in New York. Me telling him that he needed to go.

Me having the first heartbreak I've had in years.

What I left out were things that happened when I was wearing black lace, all things having to do with showers, and that I'm pretty sure I'm in love.

"Really? That's it? Just another city?"

"Yes, that's it." How is this his reaction? "Why are you not more sympathetic? Telling me that I'm going to be okay, and that I made the right decision? You know, encouraging words that a best friend should give."

"Because that's not what you need to hear."

I throw my head back and pinch my nose. "Making the choice to have a man as a best friend really sucks sometimes."

He laughs. "Katherine, I love you. I've trusted every part of my life in your hands. You've never steered me wrong. Which is why, right now, I'm not going to tell you what you want to hear, but what you need to hear."

"And what's that?"

"That you're being a proper idiot."

Wow. Apparently for Christmas Logan got me a trip to St. Lucia and a slap across the face. "Thanks. Put that on my Christmas card."

He laughs. "Well, you are."

"How? Because I told him that he shouldn't give up his dream for a woman he's known for a week? That it would be his biggest regret if he stayed in Nashville because of me and didn't go after his dream? That was the smart thing to do."

"And I'm not saying that it wasn't."

Now I'm even more confused. "If that wasn't the dumb thing, then will you tell me what it is? And none of this you guiding me so I can figure it out for myself. I have a headache and haven't had a cookie all day. I'm not in the mood for a guessing game."

"Fine," he says, though he's still chuckling. "Go with him."

"I think the signal must be bad. What did you say?"

"I said, go with him. Move to New York."

"Ha!" I yell out. "Logan, I love that you're a hopeless romantic, and that you got to marry the love of your life after knowing her for two weeks, but I've known the man for less time than that. I'm not picking up my life and moving to a new city because of a few days of good sex and the dopamine hit I'm still riding."

Yes it's more than that, but he has to know how ridiculous he sounds.

Because it is ridiculous, right?

"I can see where the hesitation comes in, but all I'm saying is that you don't have to make Nashville your home."

"I do. I have this thing called a job that you pay me to do. And last I checked, it's in Nashville, where you are firmly planted. Therefore, that's where I'll be. Plus, I like it there. I've settled in."

"But you don't have to," he says. "You're my head of public

relations. Yes, you have an office. But, tell me truthfully. How much do you have to do from that office setting?"

"I—" Shit. I see where he's going. "Okay, a lot of the work I do for you could be done remotely. But! I have other clients in Nashville. What am I supposed to do, just hop on a plane once a week?"

"Yes," he says plainly. "I don't know if you know this, but I make a lot of money. I bought a plane—a plane that *you* told me to buy—that can get me, or the people I care about, back and forth pretty quickly. Let's say from Nashville to LaGuardia."

"But—" I try to bring up a counterpoint, but it falls flat.

"Exactly." I can't see him, but I know he's grinning from ear to ear, knowing he's won this round. "All I'm saying is that you have options. It doesn't have to be all or nothing. Which I know in your Type-A Katherine brain is what you think it has to be. All I'm saying is that before either of you make a decision that you think is final, maybe talk about it. See where you both stand after you've had time to breathe."

He's right. Today's news, and the reaction to the news, was fueled by so many emotions. I jumped on Grayson for saying that he wasn't thinking about this promotion, when in turn, I wasn't thinking clearly either. I'm still firmly in the camp that he has to take this job, but...maybe it doesn't have to be all or nothing.

Maybe we can have it all?

"Kat?"

"Yeah?"

"If he's it, even if you think for a second, that he could be the one. That you found your person. The one you want to live this crazy life with? Then you figure it out. Don't let this be your regret."

Those last words smack me across the face.

Regret.

I didn't want to regret not telling him how I felt. But now...

now I know I'd regret not trying. Not fighting. Always wondering if I lose my one chance at love because of logistics.

"Thank you, Logan."

"I'll put the jet on hold. You just tell it where you want it to take you when you're ready."

"You're the best, you know that, right?"

"I do, but it's always nice hearing it again."

This makes me laugh. "Love you. Merry Christmas."

"Merry Christmas, Katherine. Now go find him."

When we hang up, I have a new feeling of optimism, but as soon as I stand up, the dread sinks back in.

Did he leave already? Once we were done crying, I got up and packed my bags. Staying in that room all day was going to be too much, so I grabbed my stuff and headed to the lobby. I figured I could wait here for my meeting with Declan and Howard before heading to the airport. I purposefully found a spot that hid me from the doors, so I couldn't see when he left. I'm now regretting that decision.

I grab my phone and bring up his number, hoping that he'll pick up when he sees my name. My heart sinks when it goes to voicemail.

"Fuck!" I yell, hoping there are no kids around. "Oh! Check in!"

I race over to the desk. "Hi, has anyone checked out of room 403?"

"And who might you be?"

In the five days I've been here, I've never seen this worker before. Just my luck. Also, I'm not being ageist, but if he has to look up something in the computer, he might need to ask me what a computer is. "I'm also staying in that room. I was wondering if the person staying with me checked out yet."

He takes his sweet time typing something into the computer. One slow finger at a time. "The only person on this room is Katherine Smith."

"Well, yes, that's me. But I was staying with a Grayson Ross as well. Has he checked out?"

"There's no Grayson Ross on the room, ma'am."

Ugh. How did he not get added? "I promise he was. Did he check out? Turn in a key? Did anyone do anything for room 403? Grayson? Santa? Scrooge? Krampus? Anyone?"

Mr. Check-In Man clearly doesn't find my panicked humor amusing. "I don't have anything for that room."

"Can you call the room for me? He's not answering his cell phone."

He seems annoyed that I'm asking him for help. Except that there's no one in line, so clearly all I'm keeping him from is his next crossword puzzle.

"Please. It would mean the world to me."

Yes. Kindness. It's Christmas. I need to not be panicked and use kindness for this man to help me.

"Fine," he says. I watch as he picks up the phone and holds it to his ear for ten seconds. "Sorry. No answer."

"Ugh!" I scream and start walking in circles. "Where are you?"

I start pacing in circles in the lobby, not sure what my next move is. Should I go to the airport? Where he's flying out of is an hour away, which isn't bad, but if he's not there, then I've lost a lot of time with no answers. And sure, I could call him later. This doesn't have to all happen today.

Except it does. Because I need him to know how I feel. The longer I don't tell him, the more this is going to eat me up inside.

"Where are you, Grayson?" I say out loud, my head thrown back in frustration when I run into someone. I wasn't looking where I was going—too lost in my scattered thoughts—which is probably how I missed the smell of his cologne.

"Hey you."

The soft tone of his voice melts me, and I instantly wrap my arms around his waist. "Hey you."

He hugs me back just as hard, each of us burying ourselves in the other.

"I tried to call you."

"I lost service for a few minutes. It's been going in and out all day."

We step away from each other, and for the first time all afternoon, I feel like I can breathe again. Which is saying a lot, because he's chosen to wear his glasses today, and with a henley, vest, and joggers.

"It's okay…can we talk? Or do you have to leave?"

He shakes his head. "We can talk."

I really should take him back up to the room, but I don't want to wait that long. "This is where I've been sitting all day."

"On a couch in the corner?"

"It felt safe," I say. "Except that it wasn't. At least from my thoughts."

"I understand," he says. "Kat, I—"

"No," I say, shaking my head. "Can I go first? There's…I need to start with an apology."

"Oh…yeah…go ahead."

I take in a breath, but reach for his hand to help give me the strength I need to put all of this out into the world.

To take the biggest risk I ever have.

"I'm sorry if I forced your hand today. That I dismissed that you didn't want the job because of me, and if I felt like I made you accept it, I apologize. It was…just everything was so sudden. And while I still think you should take the job—you don't throw away dreams—I'm wondering if…maybe…there's a way I can be a part of that dream? That is, if you still want me to be."

He doesn't say a word as his mouth dives into mine, kissing me in a way that is not suitable for the Timberline lobby. I pull away—not that I want to—but I can't get lost in his kiss when there's still so much more to say.

"I take that as a yes?"

He laughs, holding me close from behind my neck. "That's a yes. Always a yes."

I match his hold, each of us sitting close, as we take in this moment. "I don't know how this is going to work. But I *can* work remotely. I can go back and forth to Nashville and New York."

"You might not have to," he says. "I talked to Melinda today. She said that nothing is set in stone. That I can take some time to figure this out. *We* can take some time and figure this out."

I smile at his words. "I like the sound of 'we.'"

"I don't just like it. I love it."

We come back in, joining in another kiss that screams of promise and what's to come.

"So, you don't have to go to New York?"

He shakes his head. "Not yet. Not until I talk to Melinda."

"So where are you heading to today?"

"Not sure. Have any place in mind?"

"Maybe," I say with a shrug. "I hear St. Lucia is lovely this time of year."

He laughs, but the mischief is back in his eyes. "I didn't bring swim trunks."

"I'm sure we can figure something out."

"Oh, I'm sure we can."

This. This feels right. Sure, there's a ton of uncertainty, and a million and a half things to figure out. But there's one big one that's already crossed off the list: Us.

We want to try this. We want to see where this goes. And whatever is thrown at us, we're going to figure it out. Together.

"Oh good! There you are!"

Howard's voice cuts through our moment, and when we look over, we see Declan behind him.

"I'm sorry, did I miss our meeting?" I say, checking the time. "I didn't think it was for another hour."

"It's not. We were looking for him."

Grayson seems confused. "Me? Why did you need me?"

"We sent you an email asking to meet us today. You hadn't

responded, and the service has been in and out all day with our phones."

"Oh, yeah, I saw, but I didn't read it," he says. "It's okay if you're going with Kat for the campaign. I understand your decision and know you'll be in great hands."

Declan looks confused. Howard looks panicked. "Oh, that's not...Oh, dear."

"Dad...what did you do?"

Howard takes a seat in a chair opposite of Grayson and I, Declan next to him. "I saw Kat in the restaurant this morning. And...well...maybe I eluded to the fact that she was going to be getting good news today."

"And Grayson and I...let's just say a lot of things happened today, and during that, I let it slip that I was getting the account."

"Dammit, Dad," Declan says, running a hand over his jaw. "One time I want you to keep a secret."

"I didn't tell her everything," he defends. "Just a hint."

Okay, now I'm even more confused. "Is there more?"

Declan smiles. "Yes, that's why we wanted to meet with you this afternoon. And why we also wanted Grayson here."

The two of us make eye contact, clearly both lost.

"Both of you made excellent presentations," Howard begins. "Katherine, you had a way of opening our minds to things we had never even thought of before."

"And Grayson, you had such a specific plan of attack," Declan says. "Your ideas of how we could get the Timberline into national conversations really left us hopeful."

"And while I know that if we went to either of you with the other's ideas, and asked you to implement something like that, you would do it for us. But it felt wrong. We want both of you to bring your own visions to life with us."

"What are you saying?" I ask, because I think I know, but until he says it, I don't want to assume.

"We're saying, and that is, if this can be arranged with Sterling Strategies, we want to work with both of you."

Grayson starts rapidly blinking. I tilt my head back and forth. Because what?

"That's…I mean…thank you," I say. "But that's a lot of money to put forth to hire us both. Are you sure?"

Declan nods. "Dad and I agree, if you both bring to the table what we want you each to focus on, the money will make itself back almost instantly."

"We can work out the finer details after the holiday, but for now, what do you both think?"

Grayson and I share hopeful, and slightly confused, looks. Sure, this has happened before. People have different needs and different strengths; therefore they need multiple people to handle different situations. But never in my wildest dreams did I think that this could be an outcome.

"What do you think?" I whisper.

"I think it could be great," he says. "I'm not sure what this means if I take the promotion, but either way, you have the final say. Are *you* okay with this? You say the word and I back out. No questions asked."

My heart warms, knowing he'd do that for me. "I think it could be great too."

Grayson squeezes my hand before turning back to Declan and Howard. "Thank you both. Verbally, we accept. However, I've been offered a promotion with Sterling, as well. Therefore, there's a lot to think about."

"Congratulations!" Howard exclaims. "And yes, take your time and let us know. We'll talk after the New Year."

The four of us stand up, each shaking hands before Declan and Howard say their goodbyes, leaving Grayson and I standing in the lobby with a whole lot of information to process.

"That was…a lot."

He laughs as he wraps his arm around my shoulder. "I feel

like I need a debrief just to write out everything that's happened in the last four hours."

I laugh and turn to him. "Yes, but can we not debrief here? While this place has come to feel like home, I'd really, and I mean really, like to leave."

"Say less. Where would you like to do this at?"

Even though I'm ready to leave, the room does sound good for one more round. However, I get a better idea.

"I don't know if I told you, but I'm going to St. Lucia on a private jet. A jet that happens to have desks to work at. And beds to lay down in. Perfect for debriefing."

Grayson smiles as he pulls me into his arms. "Is that all it's perfect for?"

I pull him into me, our lips inches apart. "You'll just have to find out for yourself."

guide to new year's (and love) rule #105

You have to kiss someone at midnight. And if it's your forever person? Even better.

epilogue

Kat

"Okay, back the fuck up. You're meaning to tell me that in the span of two weeks, you met a guy, fucked said guy, ended up being snowed-in with said guy—who oh, by the way, hates you and you didn't know it, so then you hated him, fell for him, almost let it get away, decided against it, and then went to on a beach vacation with him, where I presume you had a shit-ton of sex?"

I've only met Logan's sister-in-law, Quinn, a few times. But every time we're around each other, I wonder why we haven't become best friends. Because this woman is a fucking hoot.

"Yeah, that pretty much covers it," I say. "Speaking of— where is he?"

I look around the living room of Logan's mansion, where all the women who have gathered here tonight on New Year's Eve have found ourselves. And we must've been into some good conversation, because now I realize there isn't an ounce of testosterone in sight.

"Where the men always end up anytime we host a gathering. The game room."

"That sounds about right," I say to Maeve, Logan's wife and the likely planner of tonight's party. I love my best friend, and if

I tell him to give me, or anyone, the shirt off his back, he'll do it in an instant. But throwing a party? Even an intimate one, for family and friends like we're having right now, is not in his wheelhouse.

Now Maeve? The interior designer who at this time last year decorated an entire mansion, and a festive party for the who's who of Nashville, in three weeks? I have a feeling this is all her doing. And that has nothing to do with the guest list.

For the most part, everyone here is related to her, including her four siblings, their partners, as well as any children that come with them. But it's not limited to the Banks family. Logan's brother, Callum, who in the eleven years we've known each other I've never met, is visiting from England. I hadn't talked to Logan since Grayson and I left for St. Lucia, so needless to say, my jaw was on the ground when I saw the tall, beefy, rugby player hanging around Logan's kitchen tonight when Grayson and I arrived.

While I was shocked by that guest, Grayson's jaw dropped when a few random professional football players passed by him and introduce themselves. One is Linc Kincaid, who dates one of Maeve's sisters. The other apparently is a man named Maddox, who Grayson absolutely fanboyed over. Apparently, Maddox didn't have plans and wanted to keep things low-key because their team, the Nashville Fury, have a game the day after tomorrow. And all he needed to hear was "video game room" and he invited himself to the party.

It's quite a mashup, but it feels right.

I've been having that feeling a lot lately. Even just thinking that makes me sound cheesy as hell, but I guess 'tis the season.

Once Grayson and I left the Timberline, we actually took the first few days in St. Lucia to just relax and learn more about ourselves. We might be on one of the wonkiest timelines ever when it comes to dating and the beginning of our relationship, but we did agree that we needed to pause for a little bit and really get to know each other. Spend time with each other.

And we did. We laid on the beach and talked for hours. Tried different restaurants. Walked, talked, and shopped. The man even got me to go out on an excursion—it was short, and I didn't need hiking boots. We had an amazing time. But sometime between our third day on the beach and the nighttime dinner cruise, we realized in the two-ish weeks we've known each other, all but two of them have been in a hotel room. It was time to get back to Nashville, and we made it just in time to ring in the new year surrounded by friends.

And, most importantly, sleeping in one of our own beds tonight, where sleeping is the last thing we do.

"Mommy! I beat them all!" We all turn to Maeve's seven-year-old son, Jayce, who is sprinting into the living room and launching himself into Maeve's lap. "They play *real* football, but I just beat them on video game football."

"I still don't think it was a fair fight." Maddox says. "The little man lives here. Unfair advantage."

The guys all laugh and give Maddox a pity back slap as they all make their way to their respective partners.

I can't help but smile as I watch Grayson and Logan walking toward Maeve and me. While I don't think I'd ever break up with someone if Logan didn't like them, his approval means more to me than anyone else's.

"Kat, I'm going to say this with all of the love in my heart… but if you fuck this up, we're done. I'm picking him."

I gasp as I stand up off the couch. "Logan William Matthews! How dare you pick him after our decade-plus of friendship."

"Wait, what's this about?" Maeve asks, joining us in the conversation. "Are we picking breakup teams already?"

Logan shakes his head. "Not at all. I don't want them to ever break up. I'm just saying, it might be a tough decision if I ever had to make it."

"You were with him for an hour. What happened in that hour that made my best friend put me on notice?"

"I didn't mean to," Grayson says as he puts up his hands in

surrender. "I just mentioned how I think video game cheat codes ruin the experience. Which led us to talking about other things that we think are sacred. Which led us to talking about movie sequels and a thousand spinoffs and remakes of classic things that shouldn't be messed with."

"Oh geez," I mumble. "Are you a comic book nerd too?"

Grayson pulls me into his side, kissing my cheek. "Big time."

I let out a groan as Maeve and Logan chuckle next to us.

"I must say, Grayson, I knew you were different right away."

"Really?" Grayson says with a smirk, adjusting us so we're now holding hands. "How was that?"

"What happened to best friend confidentiality?" I ask. "Or did one mention of fucking Spider-Man shift your allegiance?"

Logan just laughs, and honestly, I'm not mad. Logan hated Jeff, and the feeling was mutual. I don't think in the year I dated him that we ever hung out or went on any sort of double date. So seeing these two together, even if it comes with teasing at my expense, is well worth it.

"I just want Grayson to know where he stands," Logan says.

"And I just want my husband to get everything ready for the ball drop," Maeve says, pulling him away, and giving me a wink to go with it. "Let's go get the champagne ready."

Grayson and I share a laugh as Maeve and Logan head to the kitchen.

"So…."

I look up into his playful eyes. "So what?"

"How was I different?"

I let out a groan, but notice that the snow is starting to fall outside. "Come out with me?"

Grayson doesn't even have to say yes before we walk together onto Logan's expansive back patio. And because it's Nashville in December, the chill isn't too bad, despite the light snow, especially considering the weather the state had over the past week. But that doesn't stop Grayson for wrapping his arms around me to keep me warm.

I'm definitely not complaining.

"I told Logan about you after our first night together."

I can't see him, but I can feel Grayson smiling. "You did?"

Yup. And not just a smile. A shit-eating grin. "Well, I would've had to eventually, because he got a notification about the charge for his room at the Omni. But I told him before that."

"What did you tell him?"

I turn around, wanting to see him for this confession. "It wasn't as much as what I told him. It was what I called you."

"And what was that?"

"Grayson."

This seems to confuse him. "My name? Am I missing something?"

I shake my head. "Ever since I've known Logan, whenever I started seeing someone, he didn't get to know their name until it was serious. Needless to say, he knows exactly who Sweaty Hands McGee is, but he doesn't know that his name was actually Dan."

"And I didn't get a nickname?"

I shake my head. "I called you Grayson without even thinking twice about it. That's when Logan knew. And really, so did I. Even if it took me a while to admit it."

The smile on his face warms my entire body as he takes my chin in his fingers, bringing me to him for a kiss that could melt the snow around us.

We still have a lot to figure out. Grayson hasn't talked to his boss since he's returned, so his promotion might or might not happen. I might go to New York. I might stay here. Same with him. But what we do know is that whatever happens, we're going to do it together.

Because this is different. This is special. And both of us are smart enough to know that you don't throw that way.

"It's time!"

Logan's voice carries out to the patio, signaling for us to come back inside. We each grab a flute of champagne and accept a silly New Year's hat that Jayce is handing out, as we start the final countdown.

"Ten! Nine!"

Grayson spins me around to his front.

"Here's to the best year yet."

I hold up my glass to clink with his. "You and me."

"Together."

"…Three! Two! One! Happy New Year!"

The noisemakers start sounding, and there are fireworks coming from somewhere outside. But all I care about right now is kissing this man.

The one who saw me. All of me.

The one who was different.

The one I have a feeling is about to change it all.

"Happy New Year, Vixen."

I get on my tip toes to give him one more kiss. "Happy New Year, Grayson."

But wait: do you want more from Kat and Grayson? Well it's your lucky day because I have a bonus epilogue for you! Let's check in on them a little bit into the future and see how well they really do work together.

acknowledgments

It's been a few years since I've written a Christmas story and the first one I've ever written that was on my own and not part of a group project.

What did I learn? That I love writing about Christmas.

For one, it's my favorite holiday, so getting the chance to get in the mood for the season early makes my heart happy.

Secondly, I LOVE this couple.

I knew I wanted to give Kat a story way back in Single Mom's Guide to Love, and even back then, I always knew I wanted it to be some sort of a rival story. But, I didn't know Grayson until much later. But once I saw the muse of his face, and figured out that he was my kind of cocky, I instantly fell in love. And I hope you did too.

Now, to the thank yous…

Once again, the biggest thank you for this book has to go to Panera (Not sponsored. Yet). I'm convinced I can't write anywhere else, so thank you to the lovely staff, my awesome booth, the Unlimited Sip Club, and numerous Cinnamon Crunch Bagels. Y'all are the real MVPs.

To my parents. As always, you're my biggest cheerleaders even if you still have no idea what I'm doing.

Amanda, who would have thought when we met nine years ago that one day we'd be here together? Thank you for keeping my life in order. Thank you for reminding me to drink water. And thank you for being my best friend. I promise I won't fire you this week.

Kelly, you've been with me on this book journey since day one. Not only are you an amazing alpha reader, but you are an amazing friend.

To my author tribe, you make this business fun and not so lonely. Thank you to Janice and Abby for being my writing buddies every morning. To my work wife Bella for the constant cheerleading. And Julia, you keep me sane most days. Thank you for talking me off many ledges.

Kiezha…HOLY SHIT! Thank you for correcting my bad grammar habits and being an amazing editor. Michele, thank you for dotting the Is and crossing the Ts.

Corinne, I'm here because of you. If you wouldn't have given me a chance I wouldn't have started writing. You forever changed my life.

Last but not least: Readers. I love you all. Whether this was your first book by me, or you've been here since Reformation, I'm truly thankful for all of you. There are so many amazing authors you could be reading. I'm humbled that you chose me.

about the author

Known for her witty sense of humor, Chelle Sloan is a former sports editor who after completing her Master's degree in journalism, decided to become a romance author. You know, because that's the normal path to writing happily ever afters.

An Ohio native, she's fiercely loyal to Cleveland sports, is the owner of way too many — yet not enough — tumblers and will be a New Kids on the Block fan until the day she dies. She does her best writing at Panera in her magic booth. When she's not writing, she's trying to learn to bake, fixing up her condo (badly and by watching YouTube videos), or falling in love with a book.

As for her own happily every after? Maybe one day...

Stay up to date with all things Chelle & join the VIP Squad!

also by chelle sloan

THE NASHVILLE FURY, PRO FOOTBALL SERIES

Off the Record: A secret office romance

Off Track: A surprise pregnancy romance

Off Season: A second chance romance

Off Limits: A sibling's best friend romance

NASHVILLE FURY WORLD

Off the Market at Christmas: A childhood friends-to-lovers romance

LOVE ONLINE SERIES

Thirst Trap: A social media romance

Match Maker: A fake dating romance

Run Run Rudolph: A celebrity, holiday romance

ROLLING HILLS

The One I Want: A single dad / nanny romance

The One I Need: An accidental marriage romance

The One I Love: A friends to lovers romance

The One I Hate: An enemies to lovers romance

GUIDE TO LOVE SERIES

Runaway Bride's Guide to Love: A brother's best friend, age gap romance

Single Mom's Guide to Love: A billionaire, marriage of convenience romance

Roommate's Guide to Love: A small town, single dad, romance

Good Girl's Guide to Love: A fake dating, pro football romance

GUIDE TO LOVE WORLD

Vixen's Guide to Christmas (A rivals-to-lovers, one bed, holiday romance)

NASHVILLE PLAYERS SERIES

Unplanned Play: A pro football, reverse age gap, romance (Coming February 2026)